ABT

In the Foxes' Lair

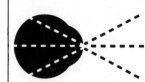

This Large Print Book carries the
Seal of Approval of N.A.V.H.

In the Foxes' Lair

Bea Carlton

Thorndike Press • Waterville, Maine

Published in 2003 by arrangement with Bea Carlton.

Thorndike Press Large Print Christian Mystery Series.

The tree indicium is a trademark of Thorndike Press.

The text of this Large Print edition is unabridged.
Other aspects of the book may vary from the original edition.

Set in 16 pt. Plantin by Minnie B. Raven.

Printed in the United States on permanent paper.

Library of Congress Cataloging-in-Publication Data

Carlton, Bea.
    In the foxes' lair / Bea Carlton.
        p. cm.
    ISBN 0-7862-4537-9 (lg. print : hc : alk. paper)
    1. Missing children — Fiction.   2. Kidnapping —
Fiction.   3. Mexico — Fiction.   4. Large type books.
I. Title.
PS3553.A736 I45 2003
    813´.54—dc21   2002190711

In the Foxes' Lair

1

The petite honey-blonde sat far back in the airport waiting room. Her midnight blue eyes, hidden behind large sunglasses, intently examined the passengers spilling into the large room. Suddenly she spied two slender women — the older one carrying a chubby blond baby. Immediately, the watching woman dropped her head so as to appear to be reading the magazine she held. Furtively gazing up through thick, black eyelashes, she followed their progress closely.

As she watched, the older woman, with ash-blonde hair and a slim, expressive face, turned green eyes upon her companion and said something. The younger girl, equally blonde and green-eyed, reached out shapely arms to take the baby who promptly wrapped his chubby arms about her neck and laid his cheek against her shoulder.

The watching woman's eyes narrowed. Her well-molded lips curled in contempt. "How touching." Her words were barely audible, but a large lady two seats away turned to stare curiously.

The blonde ignored her. Staring fixedly at the two young women and baby, she muttered, "Welcome to Veracruz, Mexico, Linn Randolph, Bobby, and Penny. May your stay be pleasant in our beautiful seaport city!" Her soft husky laugh was mocking.

Suddenly a stout, affluent-looking Mexican couple burst through the milling crowd and hurried forward. The pleasant, motherly looking woman warmly embraced Linn and Penny and exclaimed over the baby. The man picked up the women's two small bags and led the way off down the wide corridor toward the baggage claim area.

Watching until they were far down the corridor, the blonde finally stood up and followed, just keeping them in sight until they drove off in a large station wagon.

An hour later Esteban Molinas drove through a high, sculptured metal gate toward a hacienda set inside a stone wall which closed it off from the street. Curving around the back of the house, the car came to rest under a carport shaded by masses of brilliant pink bougainvillea.

"Welcome to Casa de Flores," Esteban said with evident pride, as he assisted Linn, Penny, and his wife, Alicia, out of the car.

"Casa de Flores is certainly well named," Linn said appreciatively, looking around at the flowers which grew in profusion everywhere. Radiant blossoms grew in pots, well-tended beds, and clambered up the walls of the house.

"Flowers are my wife's passion," Esteban said proudly.

A smiling, dark-skinned young man-servant came to lift their luggage out of the car. Alicia took Linn's baby into her plump arms and said in her softly accented English, "Your rooms are all ready, and I know you will want to rest before lunch." Penny and Linn nodded in agreement and followed her, Esteban, and Pablo through a hall and out into a patio-garden.

Linn drew in her breath and exclaimed, "This is simply beautiful! The house, the patio — everything!" She turned to Esteban, "Did you design and build this?"

Esteban laughed in pleasure. "I wish I could say I did. As an architect, I prefer the old style Mexican architecture myself. I was simply fortunate to obtain this old house.

We've made a lot of repairs and done some modernizing but have been careful not to disturb its natural, old-fashioned charm."

"You did a superb job as head architect on our shopping center in Corpus Christi five years ago," Linn said, "but I'm with you! These old Mexican homes have a charm that new houses do not have."

They had circled the patio on a flagstone walk and entered a wide hall. Esteban opened the first door and stepped back for Linn, Penny, and Alicia to enter. Pablo carried in their luggage and departed. Alicia crossed the cool, tastefully furnished room and flung open a door. "Here is Bobby's nursery," she said.

Linn and Penny followed her into a smaller room. Three walls were painted a pale blue, and the fourth was covered in white wallpaper, sprinkled with delightful little teddy bears.

"How absolutely gorgeous!" Penny exclaimed, her green eyes glowing.

"Alicia," Linn scolded, "you painted and decorated this room just for our visit, didn't you?"

"Yes, and I had so much fun planning it that you mustn't say a word! I'm just glad you like it."

"We love it!"

Alicia placed Bobby in the large baby bed where he lay kicking his feet and chortling happily.

"How soon will your husband and Eric arrive?" Esteban asked from the doorway.

"Clay hopes to be finished with their business in San Diego in a few days," Linn said. "You were so sweet to invite us to come early for this visit."

Esteban's dark eyes crinkled in amusement, "We'll get even with you when we accept your offer to visit your home in Idaho."

"You'd better!" Linn smiled.

A maid appeared at the door and spoke briefly to Esteban. He answered with a few terse words and then turned to his guests. "There is a call for me, so I must go. I'll see you at lunch." He left the room quickly in the wake of the maid.

"Penny, your room is on the other side of Bobby's room," Alicia said. "Come and let me show you." She opened the door, and Penny and Linn followed her into the room.

"Both yours and Linn's room open into the *corredore*. Those drapes open so you can see out into the garden." She drew back the drapes, and Penny gasped in delight.

"It's like a picture!"

Out past the open, three-sided room that circled the patio-garden, the patio fountain sparkled. Flowers, shrubs, and trees vied with each other in size and color of blossoms, colorful birds and large butterflies flitted about.

"Now I will go and let you rest," Alicia said. "There is a bathroom across the hall. *Mi casa es su casa,* as we say in our country. Make yourselves at home. Lunch will be served in about thirty minutes."

They followed her back through the nursery into Linn's room. She walked to the doorway and then turned back. "Your friends, Josie and her brother, will be arriving by dinnertime." With a quick wave of her hand, she left them.

Penny stood silent for a moment, then asked tonelessly, "Do you mean that Alfred Benholt is going to be visiting, too? I know Josie and Eric are sharing our vacation, but I did not know Alfred was coming."

Linn looked uncomfortable. "Yes, he's joining us. Do you mind?"

Penny Marshall's green eyes suddenly flamed; her pointed face paled with fury as she faced her sister.

"Yes, I do mind! You and mother connived together to get me with Alfred Benholt again! You thought his 'charm' would make me forget all about Bart!" Her well-formed lips curled with scorn and she laughed — a hoot of derision. "Well, it won't work!"

Linn stood speechless, her gold-flecked eyes filled with dismay, and her expressive slim face — so like Penny's — mirrored pain.

Tossing back her long mane of straight, silvery-blonde hair, Penny spoke contemptuously, "Get that hurt look off your face! Why shouldn't I be mad? You and mother treat me like I'm a child! I'm eighteen, remember?"

Her voice turned bitter. "I'm not surprised that mother is trying to manipulate my life, but I am surprised that you tried to help her!"

Linn spoke defensively, "Penny, no one is trying to manipulate your life. Kate and I. . . ."

"Then why didn't you — or mother — tell me Alfred Benholt was also invited to share this vacation here in Mexico?" Her voice took on a mocking note. "Alfred Benholt, the boy I was madly in love with when I was thirteen! Really, Linn, this is too much!"

Linn took a deep breath and expelled it slowly. "Okay, Penny, I'll admit Kate and I should have told you that Alfred had been invited. But so had his sister, Josie, and her husband. We were afraid you wouldn't come if you knew. We just wanted you to come away from Bart for a few weeks — to give you a chance to think through your feelings for him."

"So you invite another guy — a childhood boyfriend, no less — to keep me company while I try to sort out my feelings for Bart?" Penny said acidly.

"We didn't invite him!" Linn said sharply, striving to keep her temper in check. Penny's withering censure was getting to her. "Our host, Esteban Molinas, invited him. I imagine he thought you might enjoy seeing an old friend again."

A sneer marred Penny's face as she suggested mockingly, "Or my dear mother, Kate — or big sister, Linn — called *Senor* Molinas and suggested he invite Alfred!"

Before Linn could speak the angry words that were sizzling on her tongue, Penny continued, "Speaking of my mother, I hope she is greatly enjoying that dullard of a new husband back at the ranch in Idaho without me around to liven things up. Oh, the battles we have had!" She chuckled maliciously.

"Jake Stone thinks that marrying mother gives him the privilege of bossing me around! Well, he's beginning to learn differently! We've had some pretty nasty rounds, and I expect there will be more if he doesn't stop trying to 'father' me. What she ever saw in that dumb rancher, I'll never know!"

"Penny, if you would only give Jake a chance," Linn urged, "he is really quite a nice man. Kate loves him and that is what is important."

"But it isn't important that I love Bart!" Penny's voice climbed the scale. "Mother can have anyone she wants but I can't! Is that fair?"

Linn laid a hand on Penny's arm, but she shook it off. Tears were trembling on her eyelashes as she demanded, "Is it fair, Linn?"

Linn's anger was gone. "Penny, it isn't the same thing. Kate is a mature woman. You are very young and—" she hesitated, and then plunged on, "we feel Bart Youngblood is not good for you. He resents anything that stands for authority. It's suspected that he uses drugs. He. . . ."

"Just because Bart's tried drugs doesn't make him a drug addict," Penny defended quickly.

"It isn't only the drugs; it's Bart's whole attitude, Penny. He dropped out of college; can't hold a steady job; runs with a wild crowd He. . . ."

"I love him, and I won't stand here and let you run him down," Penny said coldly. She turned and started toward the hall.

Suddenly, without warning, a high-pitched scream shattered the stillness of the room, followed by wild sobbing. The sounds seemed to come from the courtyard of the Molinas's home. Penny turned back toward Linn, her eyes wide with alarm.

"Someone must be in trouble," Linn said quickly. She moved swiftly past Penny in the doorway and crossed the arched loggia into the sunlit patio-garden with Penny right behind her.

A small Mexican man, dressed in the garb of a workman, was kneeling on one knee in front of a young Mexican woman.

Dressed in an immaculate white cotton dress with two heavy, neat braids of black hair hanging down her back, the young woman was sitting on the edge of the ornamental fishpond sobbing hysterically while the man obviously tried to console her. He was speaking in rapid Spanish so that Linn, who understood a little of the language, could not understand them. The only two words she understood clearly were, *"Mi bebe, mi bebe."*

As Linn and Penny stopped, uncertain whether to intrude, Esteban Molinas burst from a doorway farther down the gracefully arched *corredore*, dashed across its flagstone floor and into the courtyard. His dark eyes swept the patio and then swift steps carried him to the couple at the fishpond. Laying a hand on the shoulder of the kneeling man, Esteban spoke a few quick words.

The young man jumped up and began to speak excitedly. As he waved his hands and pointed toward the entrance of the house, the young girl continued her moaning words, *"mi bebe, mi bebe."*

"What's wrong with her?" Penny, who spoke no Spanish, asked Linn.

"I'm not sure," Linn said slowly, "but it must be serious. He called the girl Luisa. Something seems to have happened to her baby. She must be a maid here, and I presume the man is her husband."

Esteban spoke a few soft words to Luisa, but she seemed to be in a state of shock and continued to moan. Esteban leaned over and shook her arm twice, once gently and then sharply. "Luisa!"

The girl lifted her wet, grief-twisted face.

Esteban spoke gently but firmly, and she stumbled quickly to her feet, wiping her face on her apron. *"Si, Senor, si, si,"* she mumbled.

"What did he say?" Penny asked.

"I don't know," Linn said. "Something about the *federales* — that's the word for the police."

Esteban said something else to the young man, who promptly put his arm about Luisa and led her across the patio toward the kitchen.

Esteban turned with quick movement, and saw Linn and Penny watching. He hurried over. His brown face with its tiny scrap of mustache was troubled.

"A most terrible thing has happened," he explained. "A few minutes ago the small baby boy of my workers, Luisa and Jorge, vanished from its bed. His grandmother was watching him while they worked. She fell asleep and when she awoke, the baby was gone. We fear he has been kidnapped."

"Kidnapped!" Linn exclaimed. "But why? Surely they would not have money to pay for its return!"

Esteban's dark eyes glinted with anger. "I suspect the kidnappers have no wish to return the child for ransom. They probably already have it sold!"

Penny gasped, "Sold! What do you mean?"

"Many babies here in the Veracruz area have vanished in the past three months, always babies of peons who have little money to hire help to find the kidnappers," Esteban said bitterly. "The *federales* have found no clue as to who the kidnappers are.

The baby is abducted quietly, sometimes chloroformed to keep it from making an outcry. Bits of cloth have been found with traces of the anesthetic. It is suspected that the babies are being sold, but no one is sure."

"To parents who want children?" Linn asked.

"We prefer to think that," Esteban said, "but there are other possibilities that are too horrible to consider. Now, If you'll excuse me, I must call the police, though I feel it is useless. No baby has ever yet been recovered." He turned and walked swiftly back into the house.

"Bobby!" Linn suddenly exclaimed and rushed back across the *corredore* and into her room. With Penny close on her heels, they charged into the small room beyond.

They dashed over to the large baby bed set in the corner. "He's fine," Penny said softly, "and asleep." Penny was often angry with Linn of late but that anger never carried over to her baby. Penny idolized him and never tired of playing or helping with him.

Bobby, formally named Robert Claydon Randolph after his father, was lying on his back, chubby arms outflung in peaceful slumber.

Linn bent over her six-month-old son and lightly touched the dark-blond hair that curled softly about his pink cheeks. "Poor Luisa," she said softly, almost to herself. "I think I would die if anyone kidnapped my baby."

2

Dr. Josie Ford and her twenty-year-old younger brother, Alfred Benholt, stepped from a taxi in front of Casa de Flores a couple of hours later, just before dinner.

Before their bags had been set out, Linn — who had been watching for them for an hour — ran out and threw her arms about small, dark-haired Josie. "It is so good to see you!" she exclaimed. "I guess it's only been a year since we saw you last, but it seems like ten!"

She released the smiling Josie to give Alfred an equally big hug. "You're in your last year of college now, aren't you?"

As Alfred replied with a grin that he was, Pablo gathered up the luggage. Linn drew the two inside to meet Alicia Esteban who hurried across the tiled floor of the vestibule, both hands extended in welcome. Her dark eyes glowing, she embraced Josie warmly and shook hands with Alfred.

"Where is Penny?" Josie asked, her dark eyes searching the room as soon as they were inside. "Alfred and I are anxious to see her."

As if waiting for her cue, Penny sauntered into the entry hall to embrace Josie warmly. Then she turned to Alfred. The wide smile on her face vanished. "Hi," she said coolly and turned back to Josie.

Linn's heart lurched as she saw the eager light in Alfred's dark-brown eyes — framed by dark-rimmed glasses — fizzle out to be replaced with a bewildered, quickly hidden, quizzical expression. The smile on his lips faded.

Suddenly, Linn wondered how wise she and Kate had been in urging Penny to make this trip. Penny's perverseness could very well ruin the vacation for everyone.

Trying to cover Penny's pointed rebuff, Linn quickly asked Alfred if he still planned to be a marine biologist. Alfred answered politely, but his eyes strayed to Penny who was ignoring him with resolute incivility.

To Linn's vast relief, Alicia summoned a female servant named Marta to take Alfred and Josie to their quarters to freshen up for dinner.

"Dinner will be served in the *corredore*," Alicia explained, waving toward the shadowed arcade that formed an open-air patio in the center of her spacious home. "But it won't be ready for another half-hour if you wish to rest."

As Josie and Alfred left with the smiling little maid, Linn spoke to Penny through tight lips. "I want to talk to you."

Penny rolled her eyes in mock horror and chuckled maliciously, "Now for the lecture from big sister!"

Linn was so angry that it took all the self-control she could muster to keep from slapping the smirk from Penny's lips. Excusing herself with a few mumbled words to their hostess, Linn led the way back to her room.

Stepping to the door of the little nursery, Linn saw that her son was playing contentedly with a string of toys strung over the crib. She pulled the door almost closed before she turned to face Penny, who was lounging in the doorway.

Penny's green eyes met Linn's wrathful gaze insolently and she spoke first, "I didn't invite Alfred! And I don't plan to entertain him!"

"No one is asking you to entertain Alfred," Linn retorted, "but you didn't have to be rude to him! There's such a thing as common courtesy!"

Penny laughed unpleasantly. "Methinks you are already regretting taking me along on this little make-Penny-forget-Bart scheme of yours. Well, you asked for it! You will regret taking me thousands of miles from the boy I love!" Spinning about, she stormed from the room, her chin tilted disdainfully.

Although the meal that followed a short while later was delicious, Linn could not have told what was served. Penny managed to seat herself as far from Alfred as possible. Not once did she look directly at him. Even when he tried to get a conversation going with her, she cut him off with a short answer. The blood surged up into his face, and he dropped his eyes in embarrassment. He didn't try again after that, and just as studiously avoided any eye contact with her.

Linn saw, with a shrinking feeling inside, that everyone had noticed Penny's rudeness to Alfred, and the atmosphere switched from a warm, friendly one to a strained, unnatural one. Before the others were finished, Penny stood up, excused herself, and left the table without giving a reason for her sudden departure.

For the next two days, Penny stayed at a distance from Alfred, and he did not try to press the issue. After the first day, everyone else seemed to accept it. Penny spent much of her time in the patio reading or caring for little Bobby while the others went sight-seeing. She was civil and even lightly friendly to everyone except Alfred — whom she ignored as if he did not exist.

Josie tried to question Linn about Penny's attitude toward Alfred, but Linn sidestepped the issue. She apologized for Penny's behavior and told Josie that Penny was having trouble accepting Kate's recent marriage as well as some other things and asked Josie to pray for Penny.

It was a difficult time, and Linn wished for the dozenth time that she had left Penny at home. She also wished for her husband and her five-year-old daughter, Pamela. How she missed them both!

She almost regretted letting Clay's mother take Pamela for the month they were to be here. But Pamela was never happier than when she was with her adoring grand-mother, and she had added her plea to Ethel Randolph's. So Clay and Linn had reluctantly agreed and left the two happily planning all kinds of adventures.

Now, as she learned that the police still

had no news about Luisa's baby, Linn was almost grateful that at least her daughter was out of danger. No one had seen anything suspicious nor anyone who did not belong to the household. The baby had simply vanished.

Linn's heart bled for Jorge and Luisa. Both had returned to work — Jorge to Esteban's coconut grove and Luisa to her part-time work as a maid in the Molinas household — but their faces were pathetic to see. The second day Luisa had come upon Linn playing with little Bobby in the patio and had burst into tears, fleeing away toward the kitchen.

Esteban had hired a private detective to search for the child, but so far there was no hint where the baby had gone. "As usual, the baby disappears as if it is lifted into heaven," he declared gloomily. "No one's baby is safe any more."

Penny heard him and asked anxiously, "Do you think an American child like Bobby is in danger?"

Esteban looked startled and then studied the wriggling little boy in Penny's arms. "I have never heard of an *anglo* baby being snatched here in Mexico, but anything is possible. We must be on our guard and never leave the child alone. The *ninos* have only been kidnapped when left alone — even briefly, in some instances."

Penny's eyes widened in sudden fear as she declared emphatically, "We won't leave Bobby alone! Not for a minute!"

3

The night was warm, balmy. The air was filled with the scent of the myriad blossoms in the patio-garden. Penny curled up in a cushioned lawn chair, drawing her long legs almost to her chin with her arms. She sighed deeply with content.

Linn had gone with the Molinas; Josie and Alfred had also gone out; Penny couldn't remember where. Tonight, Linn had taken Bobby with her, and Penny was completely alone except for the two servants, Marta and Pablo. That pleased her. She wanted to be alone to think about Bart.

Her lips curled into a dreamy smile. Linn and her mother thought that getting her away from Bart for a month would make her forget him! How wrong they were! His longish, dark, curly hair, crooked, "who cares" grin, and gray eyes that never seemed to know a serious light, were in her

28

thoughts almost constantly.

They say he's wild. Well, perhaps he is, she thought rebelliously. *Maybe that's why I love him. He's so opposite to what I have been all my life! Good old, dependable, obedient Penny, always doing what's expected! Until mother married that — that despicable man! That had changed everything!*

Kate Marshall had never looked at a man after her husband died when Penny was very small. Even though Kate was not her natural mother, she had never known any other. Linn's and Penny's mother, Linnie, had died when Penny was born. It had been childless Kate, Linnie's only sister, who had taken Penny as her own.

But Jake Stone changed all that! Penny thought angrily. *As soon as he set eyes on Kate at that church social, he had never let a day pass without calling her or coming to see her.*

I didn't like him from the first, Penny thought furiously. *He demanded all of her attention and got most of it!*

And mother gloried in the attention! Going around like a moonstruck teenager! Has it only been twelve months ago that mom met Jake? They've only been married four months, and it seems forever!

I never have a moment alone with mother anymore, she thought, her lips curling with dislike. *Jake said he wants to be a part of everything in our lives! But I don't want him to be a part of mine! It isn't enough that he has stolen my mother, but now he wants to run my life for me, too.*

Maybe that's why I like Bart so much, she thought maliciously. *Because Jake doesn't like him! Jake is so respectable! Well,* she thought defiantly, *they can do what they will, but I intend to have Bart, whether they like it or not!*

"Penny."

Penny started violently. She looked up to find Alfred staring down at her with serious brown eyes.

Straightening up in the chair, Penny said with studied malice, "Oh, it's you." She was furious. How dare he thrust his company upon her when she had shown him plainly that she did not want anything to do with him!

Alfred's jaw set grimly, and his voice took on an edge. "Yes, it's me! And I plan to find out what's eating you!"

Penny was startled at the authority that showed in Alfred's stance and words. But she schooled herself to rise languidly to her feet, look him right in the eyes, and speak with scorn, "What I do or say is none of your business! Now, if you'll excuse me." She turned to move past him.

Alfred's hand shot out and gripped her wrist. It was amazingly hard and strong! She tried to yank her arm from his grasp, but with seemingly no effort, Alfred retained his hold on her wrist. He swung her around and pinioned her other wrist.

"Let me go!" Penny demanded. "How dare you try to manhandle me." She struggled violently, but he held her easily.

Penny looked up into Alfred's grim, determined face. "I'll call the servants!"

"Call away!" Alfred said. "But I saw Pablo serenading Marta out in the front street. Neither one could hear you. You are going to talk to me whether you want to or not! I'm sick and tired of this game you are playing. You owe me an explanation!"

"And why do I owe you anything?" Penny said spitefully.

Alfred was silent for a moment while he searched her face, but he still held her wrists. His voice softened. "We were once friends — and I have done nothing to change that. But if you think I have, I deserve to know what."

Penny again struggled to free her wrists but could not. Tears of frustration and wrath sprang to her eyes. "L-let me go."

"Only if you promise to talk to me," Alfred said doggedly.

Penny struggled to pull her hands free but could not. "Okay, I promise!" she said grudgingly.

Alfred released her wrists.

She rubbed them and said sullenly, "You hurt me."

"I'm sorry," Alfred said gently. "But I had to hold you or you would have stalked off. Now, let's sit down and have our little talk."

He drew up a scrolled metal chair and straddled it with his arms across the back. Penny noticed that his lean, strong hands were tanned as if he spent much of his time out-of-doors.

Penny sank back into the cushioned chair. "It isn't really you I-I'm angry with," she said. Suddenly she felt ashamed. Pink color rose into her cheeks, and she looked down at her clenched hands, away from Alfred's direct gaze. She had been behaving abominably toward someone who had never shown her anything but friendship — and even adulation five years ago.

Penny hesitated and glanced up at Alfred through thick golden eyelashes. He was waiting calmly; his intent brown eyes never left her face.

Slightly flustered, she hurried on. "Mother and Linn put a lot of pressure on me to make this trip. I didn't want to come.

You see — I-I'm in love with a wonderful guy, Bart Youngblood." Her voice quickened, "We had planned to get married as soon as I finished high school this year at mid-term. But they don't like him. They insisted I wait at least a few weeks and make this trip — to get away from Bart and to sort out my feelings to see if they're genuine."

Penny saw sympathy spring into Alfred's expressive eyes, and rushed on, her voice turning bitter. "Mother met and married an Idaho rancher four months ago. Well, I don't like him. But no one consulted *me* about what I thought of him! And no one asked *her* to wait and see if *her* feelings were genuine!"

"You still haven't told me yet why I've been getting frostbite from you."

"Oh, I guess I haven't. I was angry because I didn't know you had been invited to keep me company while I examined my feelings for Bart."

Suddenly — incongruously, it seemed to Penny — Alfred threw back his head and laughed uproariously. At first Penny was shocked, but then began to be thoroughly miffed as he continued to laugh as if the whole thing was a big joke.

Penny stood up abruptly. "If you're just going to laugh at me, I'll. . . ."

Alfred put up a placating hand and drew

her back down as he tried to restrain the mirth that twitched at his lips. "I'm sorry," he said. "I'm not laughing at you but at this whole ridiculous situation. I, too, was coerced into coming! Big sister Josie has almost twisted my arm off at the elbow, insisting that I must come and entertain you! So you can see why this whole thing is so laughable."

Penny felt humiliated and said in an aggravated tone, "Was the thought of entertaining me as repulsive as all that?"

Alfred chuckled, not abashed in the least. "You will have to admit — entertaining you has been like entertaining an icicle!" His dark eyes twinkled. "A very lovely icicle but an icicle, nevertheless."

Penny tried to hold on to her trampled pride and hurt feelings, but the companionable, friendly grin and the mischief dancing in Alfred's eyes seemed to dissipate them in spite of herself. How tall he had become, with a lean, hard strength that was somewhat bewildering — and disconcerting. This self-assured, good-looking young man was a far cry from the awkward boy she remembered.

A faint smile tugged at her lips, then deepened into a real one. "I guess I have been acting like a complete moron," she said. "I'm sorry. But you didn't know I was going to be an 'icicle.' So why didn't you want to come? A girlfriend, maybe?" Strangely, the thought wasn't comforting.

"Well — there is this cute little redhead —" Alfred grinned. Then he sobered. "Not really. Seriously, I've been too busy getting my degree to spend a lot of time with girls. I've taken extra classes and gone summers as well as regular sessions. My brother, Joe, and Josie loaned me money so I haven't had to work and could finish faster."

"All the knowledge you collected before you got into college should have helped. You were practically an encyclopedia on marine life at fifteen!"

"Yes, it helped, but there is so much yet to learn."

"You were always so sure of what you wanted to do and be," Penny said thoughtfully. "I have never really planned to be anything, except now — to be Bart's wife."

"What does your boyfriend do? For a living, I mean," Alfred asked.

Penny hesitated. "Bart isn't doing anything right now — I mean — well, he was going to college, but he dropped out the middle of the first term. He decided to take some vocational training, welding," she hastened to say.

"Will you be married when he finishes that?"

Penny was suddenly embarrassed, and it angered her. "Bart didn't stay with welding school. He wasn't really cut out to be a welder, so he worked on a construction job for a few weeks, but they didn't pay much for unskilled work so he quit."

Alfred seemed thoughtful, and suddenly Penny could almost see Alfred's brain analyzing and assessing her prospective husband's ability to provide for a family, even though he didn't say anything. The very fact that he didn't say anything upset her and put her on the defensive.

"Everyone isn't like you," she said coldly. "It takes some people longer to know what they want to do for a living, and Bart just hasn't found what fits him yet. After all, he's only nineteen!"

"Say — I don't even know the guy," Alfred said quickly. "But he must be a great guy if you fell for him. And, I'd say a pretty lucky guy, too."

"Thanks," Penny said, pacified. "He truly is a great person, so full of fun. He's always making jokes and has everyone laughing all the time. Mother — and Jake — think he isn't ever serious, but he is when we talk about getting married and all."

"As long as you love each other and don't get married until Bart is established in a good job, I'm sure your family will learn to like Bart," Alfred said comfortingly.

"I don't think we have to wait 'til Bart has a real good job," Penny said earnestly. "As long as he has one of some kind, I'm willing to work if I need to. The important thing is that we can be together."

Alfred's face reflected his skepticism. "That's a poor way to start a marriage, Penny. And you aren't really skilled in anything either, are you? Unless a person has a skill these days, it's hard to make a living wage."

"You sound just like Mother and Jake — and Linn," Penny said in disgust. "I suppose Linn put you up to trying to talk me out of marrying Bart! Well, it won't work — so there!" She jumped up, but before she could dart away, Alfred rose also and stopped her with a firm hand on her arm.

His eyes were serious. "No one told me about Bart. What I said was meant as friendly advice from a friend." He shrugged, "What you do with it is your business, but I would still like to be friends."

Penny stood for a moment, seemingly undecided.

"For old time's sake when a skinny kid followed you about with stars in his eyes?" Alfred said teasingly. "Besides, it's going to be awfully uncomfortable around here if you continue to freeze me out."

"Okay," Penny said, "if you promise not to lecture me about how unwise teenage marriages are."

"I won't promise," Alfred said, "but I'll try." He stuck out a hand, and she grasped it, shaking it solemnly.

4

As their hands parted, a soft voice spoke near them. Penny turned to see Marta, the dark-eyed housemaid, standing a few feet away.

She spoke a few words in Spanish. Then, when she realized that they did not understand, she waved toward the *corredore* behind her.

A figure materialized from the shadows and moved toward them. It was a very attractive blue-eyed, honey-blonde. Her slim figure was clad in expensively elegant, lavender slacks and matching silk blouse. A few feet from Penny and Alfred, she spoke in a soft voice.

"I'm sorry to intrude like this. But I was so pleased to hear there were Americans visiting in Veracruz, and I was so lonely for some American conversation that I hurried right over."

Advancing, she held out a delicate white hand on which sparkled a ring of fantastic beauty; its numerous diamonds and rubies clustered about a large diamond. "I am Adella Fernandez, originally from San Diego. Welcome to Veracruz." Her dark blue eyes glowed warmly.

Penny and Alfred introduced themselves and asked her to be seated, which she did, gracefully reclining in the chair Penny had just vacated.

"And where are you from?" Adella asked, her eyes alight with interest.

The only thing that mars her beauty is that large birthmark on the left side of her face, Penny thought, trying to keep from looking at it. The dark blot extended from the corner of her left eye, down over the fine jawbone and out almost to the hairline, an irregular diamond shape about two inches in size. It was skillfully camouflaged with make-up but definitely discernible.

But her thick, dark eyelashes and exquisite features make up for that blemish, Penny decided, as she answered Adella's question. "My sister, Linn Randolph, her six-month-old son, and myself are from Idaho. Alfred and his sister, Josie Ford, are from Texas."

"And the husbands of the Mrs. Randolph and Mrs. Ford? Too tied up with business to come, I imagine. We wives of important men are almost business widows." She laughed, a throaty tinkle of empathy.

"Oh, no, they'll be here in a few days," Alfred assured Adella.

"Do the Randolphs have other children?"

"A little girl, Pamela." Penny supplied, "She's a cutie who looks a lot like her father."

"I would love to see the children," Adella gushed. "I have none of my own, and I just adore the dear little things!"

"Bobby is with his mother," Penny said regretfully. "They have gone out with the Molinas. But Pamela didn't come. She's with her grandmother back in the States."

Alfred spoke. "Could we offer you some refreshments, Mrs. Fernandez?"

"Thank you, but no. I have a dinner engagement in an hour. Have you young people seen the sights?" She stayed only a few more minutes, chatting about places to sightsee in the area. Then she rose to go.

"I mustn't wear out my welcome the first time I visit," she said with a low, tinkling laugh. "It has been pleasant talking with you. I'm so sorry that Mrs. Ford, Mrs. Randolph — and her little baby — were not present. But I'll be back and I shall hope to meet their husbands when they arrive.

"Do give *Senor* and *Senora* Molinas my regrets that I missed them! It has been quite a while since I had the pleasure of chatting with them.

"Here is my card. I'll be calling in a day or so. Perhaps you can all visit me before you return home. You must meet my husband, Luis. He's in shipping."

She moved gracefully away, calling back over her shoulder, *"Buenos noches."*

A short while later the Molinas, Linn, and Josie returned to find Alfred and Penny sitting on the loggia, sipping iced juice and talking companionably.

"Let me put Bobby to bed," Penny said to Linn as soon as she entered. "You look beat."

"You're a doll," Linn said gratefully. "I must be getting old, but I am very tired."

"We had a visitor while you were gone," Alfred said. "A lady named Adella Fernandez. She spoke as if she knew you and your wife, Esteban. Here's her card."

"She said to give you her regrets that she missed you," Penny added as she took Bobby from Linn. "Said she would call again in the next day or two."

Esteban took the beautifully engraved card, studied it briefly, and handed it to his wife. "I have no idea who this could be, do you?"

Alicia scanned the card, then looked up with a puzzled expression. "As far as I can recall, I have never heard of Adella Fernandez. What did she look like?" she asked Alfred.

"You would never have forgotten her if you'd ever seen her," Alfred said. Penny agreed, and the two described their visitor.

"I'm not sure I like the sound of this with the kidnappings going on," Esteban said. "I'll do a bit of checking on our good-looking visitor tomorrow."

"Has there been any word about the kidnappers?" Alfred asked.

"No," Esteban replied grimly. "There just isn't anything to go on. Neither the *federales*, nor Carmen, my detective, has discovered anything. That's the way it always is with these baby snatchings. No one sees anything or hears anything."

"They have to make a slip somewhere," Alicia said. "Then they'll be caught, and it will put a stop to this nightmare."

"But how many more parents will be put through this torture before it happens?" her husband said angrily.

5

Esteban called around ten o'clock the next morning from his office. Alfred and Penny had gone off exploring, but Linn, Josie, and Alicia were sitting in comfortable garden chairs, watching Bobby as he lay on a blanket, when the phone rang. Well aware of his audience of three, Bobby was putting on a show by kicking his feet vigorously, waving his arms, and chortling happily.

Alicia answered the phone. Her gentle face took on a troubled expression as she listened. After hanging up, she turned to the others. "That was Esteban. He said the city has no record of a Luis Fernandez in shipping or of an Adella Fernandez living in Veracruz. He thought, as a precautionary measure, that from now on no stranger should be allowed to enter our house or grounds.

"Esteban said he does not know what the

lady was up to yesterday, but with the recent kidnapping, he feels it wise to be extra careful," Alicia reported. "He has talked with the police, but they also have no idea who our visitor of yesterday could have been."

Linn felt the chill wind of apprehension fan through her as Alicia continued.

"And the telephone number and address that Adella gave on her fancy card were false. Esteban called the number and a funeral home answered. They knew nothing about an Adella Fernandez."

Alicia laughed. "That was pretty funny giving a funeral home's number. And not only that, she also gave the funeral home for her home address."

Josie joined in Alicia's laughter, until she saw Linn's face. "What's wrong, Linn?"

"I don't know exactly," Linn said slowly. "Maybe I'm being overly suspicious, but this visitor wishing to see us and the false address and phone number — to a funeral home, no less — leaves me uneasy. There are many other visitors to Veracruz from the United States, I'm sure. Why pick us?"

"You are right," Alicia said, her face suddenly troubled. "There are many visitors here in the winter from the United States because of our warm, tropical climate. Why, indeed, should she single you out?"

Linn's green eyes kindled. "I just don't like it." She added thoughtfully, "This Adella woman was small and dainty, beautiful, and expensively dressed. If she were not blonde and blue-eyed that could fit Bonnie Leeds's description."

"Bonnie Leeds?" Alicia asked.

"The woman who married Carlos Zorro about five years ago, when we lived in Rockport, Texas, and you lived in Corpus Christi," Josie said. "Remember? Carlos was mixed up with some stolen Mayan artifacts."

"Yes — yes, of course I remember," Alicia said. "And this Bonnie Leeds de Zorro had some kind of grudge against you, didn't she, Linn?"

"Yes, she was engaged to my husband when I met Clay. They were childhood friends. Clay broke off the engagement and married me. She never forgave me and tried once to break up our marriage and has even tried to kill me. A very vindictive, dangerous woman! But I have not seen her for five years. She is married now to Carlos Zorro so I expect she has forgotten all about me."

"I surely hope so," Josie said emphatically.

Linn sighed deeply. "I expect I'm just edgy with that kidnapper stealing poor little Luisa's baby — my heart just bleeds for her.

46

And now this mysterious woman comes calling."

"You were speaking of Carlos Zorro," Alicia said thoughtfully. "The Zorro coconut plantation — and ancestral mansion — called Guarida de los Zorros is only about thirty miles from Veracruz. Guarida de los Zorros was named by Carlos's late smuggler father. It means literally the lair, or den, of the foxes. The Foxes' Lair. Carlos's mother, *Dona* Carlota, lives there, as well as Carlos and his wife."

"That's not a comforting thought," Linn said. "I hope Bonnie doesn't learn we are visiting here. She certainly has no love for us and *is* one to hold a grudge."

As the next two days passed uneventfully, they forgot their strange visitor. Linn and Josie began counting the days until Clay and Eric would join them. Penny and Alfred remained on good terms, seeming to enjoy sightseeing together. Linn was puzzled about Penny's reversal in her attitude toward Alfred, but was extremely pleased that Penny made no further references to Bart and had dropped her sarcastic behavior.

But on Thursday, Penny had a letter from Bart. As soon as Linn saw it, she protested, "Penny, you and Bart promised not to write each other or call! This was what the trial separation was all about, remember?"

Penny was instantly on the defensive. "Well, he probably misses me!" She quickly tore open the letter and read it eagerly. "There," she said triumphantly, "read it! He says he couldn't bear to let another day pass without at least writing to me!"

Linn read it with a heavy heart. Bart wrote only two pages, but the letter was filled with words of love, undying devotion and longing for Penny to come home. He said he didn't have a job yet but was trying to find one. He was spending a lot of time with his friends, he wrote, so the time would pass faster.

Linn wondered if this vacation away from Bart had not strengthened Penny's and Bart's bonds rather than helped the situation. She prayed earnestly for them when she retired for the night, finishing with:

"And, Father, although Kate and I feel Bart is not right for Penny, you know what is best. Perhaps we are wrong, and Bart will settle down and make a good husband. But, Father, I know it will be hard if they marry before Bart has a good job. Please help them to see this."

She tried to put Penny in God's capable hands, but it was a long time before she slept. Parading through her mind were the stories she had heard of happy-go-lucky Bart. Into one thing after another from which his doting mother extricated him — one way or the other: drug parties, and escapades at high school for which he had twice been suspended. And rumor said — but Bart denied — that he had not quit college but had been expelled for peddling marijuana on the college campus.

"Dear God, please protect Penny from this marriage if it wouldn't work," were Linn's last whispered words, as she drifted into sleep.

6

Alfred left the house early the next morning. A friend of Esteban's had invited him to go out for a day of deep-sea fishing. Alfred asked Penny if she wanted to go, but she declined. Fishing was not something she enjoyed. Alicia, Josie, and Linn decided to do some shopping.

"I'll stay here and keep Bobby," Penny told Linn as they ate an early lunch. "I'm reading a good book anyway."

"If Penny wants to keep Bobby, why don't you let her?" Alicia urged Linn. "You don't have to worry about them being alone. Marta and Pablo are here, so it's perfectly safe. They have orders to not let anyone in."

"Okay," Linn told Penny, "if you're sure you don't want to go with us. But do watch Bobby carefully. This kidnapping thing has me a bit uneasy."

"I'll not let him out of my sight," Penny promised.

After everyone had gone, Penny put Bobby in his stroller and pushed him along the patio-garden paths, enjoying the flower-perfumed air and sun-drenched garden as much as Bobby did. She chatted to him as if he could understand her every word, and he gurgled and cooed in return.

"*Casa de Flores* — House of Flowers! I would like to own a place like this," she told Bobby companionably, as she admired the well-kept beds and huge clay pots of blossoming plants and shrubs. Bees, insects, and birds hummed, chirped, and sang around them.

Pablo was working somewhere inside; she could hear his cheerful whistle. Now and then she heard a quick bubble of laughter and knew Marta had paused in her unhurried duties to speak a few words to her Pablo. Alicia had said the young couple planned to be married next month but would continue to work for them.

Penny stopped for a moment, took Bobby out of his stroller and carried him over to the three-foot-tall, decorated wall of the fishpond. Perching on the wall, she tried to show Bobby the gold and black fish that swam lazily in the clear water, amid the colorful rocks and greenery. But Bobby was not interested in fish; he wanted to get in the water. When she let him dip his hands in the water, he slapped the water and laughed in delighted surprise when it splashed up into his face.

Returning him to his stroller a few minutes later, Penny continued pushing him about until he grew drowsy. Then she took him to his nursery and put him to bed. Almost instantly, he was asleep, curled up around his favorite toy, a soft, stuffed white kitten.

"You are adorable, Robert Claydon Randolph!" Penny said fondly, as she stood looking down at him. "When Bart and I get married, I hope our first baby is a son and that he looks just like you! I would name him after Bart — Bart, Junior.

"I wonder what Bart's middle name is?" she mused. "In fact, Bart is probably short for something, like Clay is for Claydon."

Picking up her mystery book, she walked over to a large comfortable rocker and curled up. But the thoughts of Bart were more pleasant than reading. A picture of his dark curly head, mischievous dark eyes, and slow, crooked grin rose in her mind. Suddenly, she wanted to see him so badly that it hurt.

The thought that came into her mind, she pushed away at first, but it stubbornly returned. *Why not call Bart?* The baby was sleeping soundly, and Marta and Pablo were nearby so there was no real danger in leaving him for a few minutes.

"I really shouldn't though," she said aloud. "I promised Linn I wouldn't call or write Bart while I'm away on this trial separation trip. I hate to go back on my promise — but . . . ."

A little dagger of anger thrust itself into her consciousness. Clay had called Linn nearly every day and Eric had called Josie almost daily, too. The dagger thrust of anger went deeper. *What right had Linn — or anyone — to demand that she not call the one* she *loved?* Anger exploded into full-blown fury. She would call Bart whether Linn liked it or not!

Besides, Linn would never know! She would call Bart collect. Linn was not due back until late that evening so there was plenty of time.

Walking out into the hall, she listened to see where Pablo and Marta were. She heard them in the kitchen, not far away. By the click of cups, the soft laughter, the scent of coffee and *espanadas,* a fruit-filled tart that was a favorite in the household, she realized that the two were taking full advantage of the absence of the mistress of the house.

Running lightly down the hall, Penny sought out the formal parlor. It was seldom used, and she was unlikely to be disturbed there. It took only a few minutes and she was talking to Bart!

He was delighted to hear her voice, and Penny lost all sense of time and place as she listened to Bart's teasing voice and hilarious stories. *He could make even sweeping a floor funny,* she thought fondly.

"Say," Bart's lazy drawl came over the phone, "guess what? Jake, your new father, offered me a job and even a little house to live in out on his ranch."

"He did? That will be great! Now we can get married right away!" Penny said excitedly.

"You didn't think I'd take a job on a ranch?" Bart asked incredulously. "I can do better than that!"

"B-but you wouldn't have to work there forever," Penny said persuasively. "Just 'til you get a better job."

Bart was silent for a moment. "Naw, I decided to wait until something better turns up. Mom's not throwing me out yet!" He laughed. "Dear old dad almost did when I turned down that job, but mom wouldn't let him. She agreed that I could do better than be a flunky on a ranch. Said she didn't want me smelling like a fertilizer plant all the time."

For some reason Penny's heart sank down into her toes, and her stomach felt a little sick. Was the family right? Did Bart really *not* want a steady job? Jake had plainly stated that he thought Bart was dodging any kind of responsibility. This new development would lend credence to Jake's argument!

"Maybe you don't really want a job — or to get married!" It popped out before Penny realized what she was saying.

"Baby! Of course I want to get married! But I sure don't want you to be the wife of a ranch hand! I want better things for you — and for me! You do understand, Penny, baby? I want us to have a good time! Time for parties and having fun! Ranchwork is from dawn 'til night, I've heard, and dirty, hard work. I just don't think I'm suited to that. I've got a good brain, and I plan to use it to make big money to buy you pretty things and all! Don't you see?"

When she hesitated, Bart rushed on. "I love you, Penny! I want what's best for *you!* You know that, don't you? I love you more than anything in the whole world!"

Bart's voice was warm and close and caressing against her ear. Penny's doubts melted, as they always did. "Yes, I know you do, Bart."

Suddenly she realized they had been talking a long time! — and on his mother's phone bill, too! "I really must go," she said reluctantly. "I'm babysitting Bobby, and I'd better go check on him."

She hung up the phone and walked slowly back to the little nursery adjoining Linn's room. Hugging Bart's husky endearments to her, she entered the room dreamily and moved to the crib.

Then the dream shattered into a million, quivering bits. Bobby was not in his crib!

Wildly and incredulously, she stared about the room before she screamed in terror for the servants. Within seconds, Marta and Pablo were both in the room. Quickly grasping the situation, Marta ran toward one entrance and Pablo the other, searching the area with horrified eyes. Running out into the street, they looked in every direction.

Her heart constricted with terror and fear, Penny ran from room to room, hoping that someone in the household had returned and taken Bobby from the crib.

Rushing back, Pablo and Marta joined her in searching every room and the patio. In a few minutes they met back in the nursery with empty hands and stricken faces. Penny burst into a torrent of wild weeping as she knew with terrible certainty: Bobby had been kidnapped!

7

Still smelling of pastries, dark-haired Marta put her arms around Penny and tried to comfort her. But Pablo, waving his hands, said urgently in broken English, "Pliz, *Senorita* Peenny, you must call *Senor* Molinas, *ahora mismo!*"

Penny tried to take control of her emotions but could not. She collapsed, crying hysterically, into Marta's arms again.

Rolling his black eyes upward in consternation, Pablo charged off down the hall to a telephone.

Esteban's secretary answered and quickly put Pablo's call through to Esteban. Pablo, talking so fast that Esteban could scarcely understand him, explained that Bobby was missing.

For a moment Esteban was too deeply shocked and distraught to speak. When he could speak again, he asked if Pablo had seen anyone in or about the house.

"No one, *Senor!*"

"Did you go out into the streets around the house?" Esteban asked.

"*Si, si!*"

"Did you see anyone who looked suspicious?"

"No, *Senor*. I ran out the back entrance and saw only an old man with a donkey load of baskets and your fat neighbor taking her little dog for a walk. Marta went out the front way, and there were only two *muchachos* playing ball in the street."

"Did you ask them if they had seen anyone run out of the house?"

"*Si,* and so did Marta," Pablo said quickly, "but they all said they saw no one."

"Has *Senora* Randolph been told yet?"

"No, I thought you should do that, *Senor* Molinas. She and *Senoras* Molinas and Ford are downtown. Only the little *Senorita* Peenny is home. And she is very upset, crying until she cannot talk. *Mucho, mucho* distressed, *Senor.*"

"I'll call the police, Pablo, and then see if I can locate the ladies. You and Marta stay with the *senorita* and answer any calls that come in," he instructed and hung up.

It took an hour for Esteban to locate the ladies. Unable to find them by phone, he finally got into his car and drove to an open market that his wife often frequented. As he hurried through the crowd, his thoughts tumbled in complete turmoil. *How could he tell Linn that her child had been kidnapped?* It would be the hardest task of his entire life.

Finally, hot, tired, and almost ready to collapse himself from mental anguish and his mad charging through the market, he saw them sitting at a little table sipping cool drinks.

Alicia saw him coming and said something to Linn and Josie before rising to wave a welcome. Then she saw his expression and the smile on her plump, pleasant face disappeared. She hurried to him, put a soft hand on his arm, and said anxiously, "Esteban! What's wrong?"

"It is Linn's baby," Esteban said softly, "let us go back to the table."

Both Linn and Josie wore worried expressions on their faces when Esteban and Alicia hastened to the table.

Linn saw Esteban's eyes go quickly to her and panic rose in her throat, threatening to suffocate her. Half rising, she asked, "Has something happened?"

"Please sit down," Esteban said. "I don't know how to tell. . . ."

Linn's face blanched as white as the clouds floating high in the sky above as she choked, "Bobby! Something has happened to my son!"

"I'm sorry, Linn — your baby is missing. But. . . ."

"No — no!" Linn's face contorted with pain and grief as she reached across the table and grabbed Esteban's hand. "Where? How — could that be? Penny always watches him so carefully."

Esteban shook his head slowly. "I'm not sure, but from what Pablo said, she left him briefly to make a call and when she returned, he was gone."

Anger lanced across Linn's grief-ravaged face. "Bart! There is no one that Penny would call except for that — that no-good playboy! She left Bobby a-alone and now he's g-gone." She sank back upon the bench, sobbing uncontrollably.

Josie put her arms about Linn and said gently, "You mustn't blame Penny, Linn. She loves Bobby dearly and would never let harm come to him intentionally. She will be devastated and will blame herself."

Esteban leaned forward. "*Senora* Ford is right. Pablo said the young lady was crying hysterically. He said she could not have been gone from the room long. He and Maria

61

were nearby, and they didn't hear or see any-one come in."

Linn continued to cry heartbrokenly.

Esteban spoke urgently. "Linn, you must pull yourself together. We should go home as quickly as possible and see what can be done to find your son."

Linn raised herself, moving in slow mo-tion as if she was barely in control of her muscles. She groped in her purse for tissues and wiped her eyes. "Y-you're right, we must go." She took a deep, quivering breath. "I'm okay. Have the p-police been called?"

"They should be at the *hacienda* now," Esteban said briskly, "and I assure you that none of us will rest until we find little Bobby!"

But as Linn turned and began walking toward their parking place, she choked and tried to stem the flood of tears that once more washed down her cheeks. She was re-calling Esteban's words of a few days ago when Luisa's baby had disappeared. *No baby has ever yet been recovered.* Linn stum-bled and would have fallen if Esteban had not steadied her with a strong arm.

"I don't think I could bear it if I never saw my b-baby again," Linn sobbed. "I would rather be dead!"

8

When the horrible fact registered that Bobby really was gone, Penny had almost gone out of her mind. Her first thought was that she was totally to blame. How could she ever face Linn and tell her that she, Penny, had broken her promise and left Bobby alone to call Bart — another broken promise!

"How could I have done such a thing?" she sobbed wildly, over and over. "God is punishing me for the terrible way I have been acting the past few months," she moaned. "I know He is.

"And what about poor little Bobby? Why did they kidnap him? What will become of him? Will someone hurt him? Oh, God, please don't let anyone hurt him! Punish me anyway you like, but don't let him suffer! I deserve to be punished, but, oh God, not this way! Please help us find him, Father

God, and I'll do anything you want me to. I promise I will! Anything at all!"

Marta stayed with her, trying unsuccessfully to console her while Pablo watched for Senor Molinas. As soon as his car appeared, he swung open the wide entrance gate. Esteban had hardly brought the car to a stop when Linn was out and running for the door.

"*Senorita* Peenny and Marta are in your room, *Senora*," Pablo said as she passed him.

Linn dashed down the hall and burst into her room, the others close behind. As she entered the room, Linn saw her sister lying on her bed, her face hidden in a pillow. Unaccustomed anger flared fiery-hot in her heart, and suddenly she hoped Penny was suffering severe anguish. Penny had broken her promise to protect and watch over her baby!

Then Penny rolled over and sat up. Her long, silvery-blonde hair was in disarray, and her eyes were so puffed from crying, they were almost swelled shut. Penny whispered through trembling lips, tears running unheeded down her haggard face, "I'm sorry, Linn. It's all my fault. I'll never forgive myself, I. . . ."

Linn crossed the room swiftly; sitting

down on the bed, she gathered Penny into her arms.

"There, there," she soothed, "what is done, is already done. You never meant this to happen." Oblivious to the others, Linn rocked Penny as she would have Bobby. Tears flowed down her cheeks, mingling with Penny's, but her voice no longer held a hopeless note.

"We'll find Bobby. The Lord will help us. I'll call Clay, and he and Eric will come. Praying together and working together, we'll get our baby back. You'll see."

The others tiptoed from the room, leaving the two alone.

Esteban softly drew the door closed, and they walked out into the cool arcade. "Where are the police?" he asked Pablo in an irritated voice.

"I do not know, but they promised to come," Pablo said worriedly. "They said there was another baby kidnapping about an hour before this one happened. Several of the *federales* were already over there. But someone is to be sent here."

"Whose was the other baby that was stolen?" Alicia asked quickly.

"The baby of a field worker," Pablo answered. "No one we know."

Esteban's brow furrowed, and he stroked

his little mustache thoughtfully. "This is very strange. All the other kidnapped babies have been from very poor Mexican families. Why have they taken one *anglo* baby — and from a wealthy family?"

"Perhaps they will ask a ransom for Bobby," Josie suggested. Her face brightened. "If only that is the case, and we can get him back unharmed!"

"Perhaps," Esteban said, "but I wouldn't count on it. I'm wondering if this is aimed at the Randolphs personally. I keep thinking of that woman who came the other day. She took nothing from the house. Marta was sure of that because she escorted her in and out again. What was her purpose in coming here? She was wearing diamonds and expensive clothes, so it's doubtful if she is in need financially. Could she have come to see if Linn Randolph was really a guest here? And to see if she had a child?"

9

Esteban turned to Josie. "Did Penny or Alfred mention if this Adella asked questions about the Randolph family?"

Josie's fine, dark brows drew together in concentration. "I believe so — yes! Penny said she asked where Clay and Linn lived, if they had children, and what business they were in. Even when Clay was coming here. I remember thinking it was strange she asked so many questions about the Randolphs and nothing about Alfred, Eric, and I. But why all the interest in Linn and Clay?"

"I don't know," admitted Esteban. "It's a feeling."

"I am very worried about Linn," Alicia said. "That baby is so dear to her."

"We will just trust God to help us and to bring Bobby back," Josie said. "It seems He is our only hope, now."

"Yes-yes," Esteban said quickly, obviously

uncomfortable at the thought that a higher power would intervene in man's paltry affairs.

A few minutes later, Linn and Penny came out into the loggia. Penny's face was still swollen, but she had washed away the tearstains and combed her hair. Dressed in a simple white and red peasant blouse and wide skirt to match, her long hair hanging loose, she looked about thirteen. And thoroughly chastened and subdued.

"May I use your telephone?" Linn asked. "I must locate Clay immediately."

But after several calls, Linn discovered that Clay and Eric had finished their business early and had already started for Mexico. He had left a message for her at his last hotel. Somehow he had not been able to get a call through to her.

The message stated that Clay and Eric had changed their plans. They had rented a small motor home and were driving through Mexico to Veracruz by way of Baja. Since they were close, they had decided to see the great gray whales off the coast of Baja and do some deep-sea fishing as they traveled.

"I'll call you Saturday evening around five, Linn," the message had concluded. "Love you and miss you much, Clay."

"That's a whole day away!" Linn exclaimed. "And after he calls, he will still have to find a way to fly here and that will take time. He may not even be near an airport! What am I going to do?"

"We are already doing what we can," Esteban assured her. "I have alerted my detective and he will be here soon, as well as the police. There was another baby kidnapping in Veracruz just before your baby was abducted. It has delayed their answering our summons."

Linn's face again contorted with pain. "It seems the whole world has gone mad! Who is stealing our babies?" Her voice broke and she hid her face in her hands. Josie put her arms about her and led her to a chair.

"Let's call Kate," Josie said. "She knows how to pray and that's what we need most right now. Don't lose your faith, Linn. Remember, God knows where Bobby is, and He is able to take care of him. Let's pray right now, and then we'll call Kate."

Without further words, Josie bowed her head. With her arms still about Linn, she prayed softly and confidently, asking God's guidance, protection for Bobby, and for God to bring him safely back to them.

Esteban did not bow his head. He watched Josie, and an awe settled over him. The little lady doctor, her small dark head crammed with so much scientific knowledge, actually expected to get an answer from her prayer!

Hearing a faint sniff, Esteban glanced over at his wife. She was wiping her eyes. Suddenly, for some inexplicable reason, Esteban felt a prickle in his own eyes. He turned away, not wanting anyone to see his furtive dabbing with his handkerchief.

What had come over him? Was he — Esteban — skilled architect and astute businessman, letting this prayer thing get to him? He certainly did not believe God — if there was one — would actually intervene, in answer to a few spoken, mortal words. Preposterous! But as Josie finished praying, strangely, he longed to believe!

The sharp ring of the telephone broke into Esteban's musings, and he went to answer it.

Alicia rang the bell, and a maid came quickly in reply. It was Luisa. "Bring us some cold pineapple juice, please," Alicia told her in English.

"Si Senora," Luisa replied. Then as she moved toward the door, she hesitated. Looking at Linn, she walked over to her. Shyly, her plain face distressed, Luisa said, *"Senora* Randolph, I am so sorry — about your leetle baby." Her velvet-black eyes filled

70

with tears, and she laid a small brown hand on her own chest. "My heart hurts for you. We are both mothers who have lost our *ninos*."

Too deeply touched for words, Linn stood up and put her arms around the little *criada* and hugged her fiercely. Then Luisa went quickly away.

Shortly afterward, the *federales* came. The dapper, uniformed captain, Juan Sanchez, was sympathetic but offered little encouragement. "These kidnappers are very professional," he said in perfect English. "They have never yet left a clue of any kind. No one sees them or hears them. One of my men found a rag near your home with traces of chloroform on it."

Linn shuddered in horror. "What if they used too much?" she asked. "Wouldn't it harm the baby?"

"That's unlikely," the captain said. "A professional would be careful that the baby was not harmed. A dead child would be of no value to them."

"What do you think they are doing with the children?" Josie asked.

"I really cannot say for sure," the captain replied, "but we presume the babies are being sold to childless parents who are willing to pay a big price and aren't particular where they come from. Black market babies are a lucrative business."

When the police left, Linn put through a call to Kate in Idaho. Kate was extremely concerned and could scarcely talk for crying.

Jake got on the other line as soon as he learned that Bobby had been kidnapped. "We won't let them get away with this," he stated emphatically. "Kate and I will be there as soon as we can get a flight. We'll find your baby, Linn!"

"I appreciate that so much, Jake," Linn replied, "but I doubt that you could do more than is being done. There just isn't anything to go on yet."

"We'll turn over every rock in Veracruz, if necessary," Jake said obstinately. "Those dirty baby stealers are only human, so they're not infallible. They'll accidentally drop a clue somewhere, and we'll find it. God's on our side! Don't you forget it, girl!"

"I'm not forgetting," Linn said a little faintly. *Jake is a little over-powering at times,* she thought, *but he has a good heart.*

Penny was on another phone in the house and heard the whole conversation.

When Linn hung up, Penny came tearing into the room, her green eyes shooting sparks. "See what I mean! Jake Stone imagines himself a John Wayne coming to the rescue! He'll come flying down here, try to take over everything, and get in the way of the police and everybody else. He'll make himself a complete nuisance!"

Although Linn agreed with Penny that Jake *would* likely get into everyone's hair, she answered with a slight smile, "Maybe we need a John Wayne! Certainly neither the police — nor Esteban's detective, Carmen — have turned up anything yet."

"All that self-styled hero will do is get crossed up with the Mexican police!" Penny prophesied darkly. Her lip curled with contempt. "I hope he does, and they put him in his place good! Or throw him in a Mexican jail for awhile! Maybe that would puncture his big red balloon where he stores all that hot air!"

"Penny," Linn scolded gently, "give Jake a chance! He means well."

"I mean well, too," Penny said venomously. "I mean to get him out of my life — and mother's, too, if possible!"

Knowing it was useless to argue, Linn dropped the subject of Penny's stepfather as Alfred walked into the house and had to be told of the kidnapping.

After a late dinner — a dinner no one ate much of — everyone retired to their rooms for the night.

Several times after she went to her room, Linn found herself walking into Bobby's room, almost holding her breath with anticipation. Surely he would be there this time!

She paced the room and talked to God. But peace was slow in coming. She had gone through some hard places, but this was the hardest yet. How could she ever survive if Bobby was not found? She choked back a sob.

How do parents who lose children this way ever pick up and go on with their lives? she thought. *I don't see how it's possible. Wouldn't they always be watching for him — in someone's arms, in strollers in the park, in the yards they passed? Somewhere, someone had their baby and they could happen upon it anytime. They must be forever looking — and never finding!*

Linn forced the morbid thoughts from her mind. *I must dwell on God's promises,* she thought. Picking up her Bible, she turned to a favorite verse in the 34th Psalm. "The angel of the Lord encamps around those who fear Him, and rescues them."

With her finger still upon the verse, Linn closed her eyes and prayed earnestly, "Father, I accept this verse as your promise to me as your child. Both Clay and I trust in you and your protection for our little Bobby. I believe your angels are camped around

Bobby right now, and you will deliver him."

What if Bobby is already dead? The terrible thought cut its tearing, searing, jagged path straight into her heart. A sob rose in her throat. *Could that be God's will?* Almost frantically, she tried to read the verse again, but tears blurred her eyes. If only Clay were here!

Linn closed her eyes and willed herself to be calm. Clay was not here but God was! Whether she felt His presence or not, His word said He was here with her, and He was! And He was with Bobby!

Her inner struggles were interrupted by a soft knock at her door, so soft she wasn't sure if it was real or her imagination. Going to the door, she asked hesitantly, "Is someone there?"

"*Si, Senora* Randolph, it is Luisa," a soft voice whispered.

Linn opened the door. Luisa stood there, her dark eyes wide with suppressed excitement.

"Come in," Linn invited, her heart suddenly constricting with both fear and hope. Luisa had some kind of news, of that she was certain. It was written vividly on Luisa's face.

The little maid glided into the room after darting a furtive look toward each end of the hall.

"Won't you sit down?"

"No," Luisa said softly. "I have a message for you from one who has news of your baby."

At Linn's quick indrawn breath, Luisa put a warning finger to her own lips. "You must promise to tell no one that I was here, or I can tell you nothing."

"I promise," Linn assured her breathlessly. "Tell me who sent you and what they said to tell me."

"I cannot tell you who gave me the message. I do not even know, I did not see her. But it was a woman — she spoke from the shadows. You are to follow me — now — out through the back gate. You must come alone and tell no one. The woman is waiting for you nearby in a car."

"What does this woman want of me? Does she want money for the return of my baby?" Linn asked.

"That I do not know. She just said she wishes to speak with you about your baby."

Linn hesitated. Little warning bells of alarm were ringing frantically in her brain. She could be in real danger of robbery or — or of anything. This unknown woman might just be taking advantage of Linn's calamity to get money from her or even to kidnap *her* for ransom.

"I don't think it is wise to go out there alone and in the dark," Linn said slowly. "How do I know this woman really knows anything about my baby?"

"The woman said this would prove to you that she has news of your son." Luisa pushed a small envelope into Linn's cold hand. "She also said you would never see your baby again if you do not come to him now."

Linn tore open the envelope with trembling fingers and drew out the contents. The envelope contained a strand of soft, dark-blond hair wrapped in a six-inch square of blue cloth with little white boats sprinkled on it. Linn instantly recognized both. The hair was Bobby's, and the cloth was cut from the little shirt he had been wearing when he disappeared!

10

Linn's knees suddenly lost strength, and the room seemed to go into a slow spin. Dimly, as through a whirling mist, Linn saw Luisa's anxious brown face.

Luisa reached out a steadying hand. "Are you all right, *Senora* Randolph?"

The room tilted and righted itself and tilted again. Linn closed her eyes and stood very still. Slowly, the room stopped its rolling. She opened her eyes. Luisa stood in front of her, both small, strong hands upon Linn's shoulders.

"I'm f-fine now," Linn said, "and I'm ready to go. No, wait I could write a brief note, couldn't I? Just to tell the Molinas I've gone to meet someone with knowledge of the baby."

Luisa considered a moment, "Well, the woman did not say you couldn't. Write it quickly. We must be going."

Linn snatched a piece of stationery from a small desk and wrote a few succinct words.

I have gone out back to see a woman who has news of Bobby. Linn.

Luisa quickly perused the note, laid it on Linn's bed and hurried Linn to the door. Urging Linn to walk softly, she peered down the hall both ways; then Luisa moved swiftly down the short hall to a heavy oak door. Drawing a key from her dress pocket, Luisa unlocked the door and drew Linn outside.

As she followed Luisa down a shadowy alley, for the first time Linn wondered how Luisa had become involved in the kidnapping of little Bobby. This woman had also lost a baby the past few days — presumably to the same kidnappers. Suddenly an idea flashed into her mind.

"Luisa. . . ."

Luisa stopped quickly and whispered, "Please do not talk. We might be heard."

But Linn grabbed her arm and whispered, "Luisa, what are you getting for bringing me out here? Your baby back?"

Luisa stood very still, and Linn could not see her face in the shadows. Then she said very softly, "The woman promised you would not be hurt before I would agree to bring you a message. That is all you need to know. Now come, before she decides we are not coming."

She started off again, and Linn almost had to run to keep up. Obviously, Luisa wanted to be rid of this chore as quickly as possible. At the end of the alley, Luisa stopped suddenly and drew Linn back under the underhang of a tall oleander hedge until a car passed. Then, after looking both ways, Luisa gripped Linn's arm and led her quickly across a dimly lighted side street and into the dark mouth of another alley. Releasing her arm, Luisa whispered, "Stay close beside me," and moved on more slowly.

Linn's apprehension was mounting. Had she been very foolish to come here? Perhaps she should turn back. She slowed her steps, but at that moment Luisa stopped and pointed ahead into the shadows.

"There! In the car."

Linn stared into the semi-darkness and could just barely see the outline of a car. There were no lights or sound, and Linn felt a quiver of fear travel quickly down her spine.

"You are coming with me, aren't you?" Linn asked. She turned back toward Luisa, and her heart almost stopped beating. Luisa was gone! She was completely alone! Frantically, Linn looked all around her, but Luisa was nowhere to be seen, and not even the sound of a footfall broke the stillness.

Linn was suddenly terribly afraid. How utterly foolish she had been to come here — away from all help. Turning, she ran swiftly back the way she had come, toward the pale street lantern that cast an uncertain light into the side street she had traversed a few short minutes before.

Even as she fled, though, she heard a car engine spring to life and the whisper of tires in the gloom behind her. Raw terror put wings to Linn's feet. She was almost to the side street when the dark form of the car slipped by her and spun to block her path.

Before Linn could dart around the vehicle, the door yawned open. A dark figure leaped out and grabbed her. She opened her mouth to scream but a large gloved hand instantly covered it, almost smothering her. She fought to free herself, but the dark hulk who held her just tightened his grip. Her face brushed against his jacket. He smelled of strong tobacco, leather, and sweat.

Finally, realizing it was futile, Linn stopped struggling, aware that she should try to conserve her strength for whatever lay ahead.

Without a word, the big man pushed her into the back seat of the car and closed the door. The voice of another man spoke from the back seat. It sounded vaguely familiar, Spanish-accented, and broken.

"Try to geet away, and you weel be sorry."

The man who had captured her slid into the front seat. Instantly, the car backed up. With lights still off, it swung out into the side street, hesitated briefly, and then moved swiftly down the road.

Although the street was poorly lighted, Linn could now see that the driver of the car was a woman. Leaning slightly forward, Linn spoke to her.

"You must be the woman who sent Luisa to me. Who are you? Where are you taking me? Where is my baby?"

For a long moment no one spoke. Then there was a light patter of laughter, and a low, throaty voice answered, "I am Adella. You wanted to see your baby. I am taking you to him."

"Why did you kidnap him?"

There was another pause before the low, throaty voice answered. "You will know soon enough." A hardness had crept into the voice. "Now shut up and let me drive!"

They turned into a modest neighborhood and Adella switched on the car lights. Small, tile-roofed houses lined the narrow street. Linn looked up into the mirror above the driver but could not see the face of the woman. She wore a big hat, tilted to hide her face.

Linn turned her head slightly so she could see the other occupant of the back seat. He, too, wore a large hat, pulled low to throw deep shadows over his face. The back of the big man's head in the front seat was faintly discernible, but his big ears, bulky bull-like neck, and bushy head did not look familiar.

It seemed to Linn that they traveled for hours but later she wasn't sure. Tired and drained, she kept slipping in and out of fitful naps. But she awoke when the car finally stopped. The big man pulled her from the car without speaking — and pushed her ahead of him. She stumbled over uneven ground toward a large, low building.

Suddenly the moon slid from behind a cloud and Linn saw with a shock that they were at an airport. She could now see two small airplanes, a larger one, and a helicopter — toward which they walked.

Panic froze Linn's brain. How would anyone ever find her! Almost as if they had a mind of their own, Linn's arms jerked from the grasp of her big captor, and she was free, running like a scared deer. Tree-covered hills crowded close on their side of the airport. Toward these she fled as she heard yells behind her and the slap of pursuing feet.

But Linn's sandals were not made for running. She was nearing the first of the trees when the strap on one of them broke, sending her plunging painfully to the ground.

Ignoring the pain, Linn scrambled to her feet, but her flight was halted in mid-stride by her pursuer, the smaller Mexican man. He grabbed her right arm causing her to cry out. But he only took a firmer grip and began pulling her roughly back toward the 'copter, spitting out angry Spanish in rapid bursts.

Tears of pain ran down her cheeks as the man forced her along rapidly. From the way her knees burned and throbbed, Linn knew they must have lost some skin, and her right arm — which had broken her fall — felt like it was sprained. Finally she gasped out, "Please let go of my arm. You are hurting it awfully! I — I think it's sprained."

The man dropped her arm so suddenly that she nearly fell as he began pushing her along instead, shoving or prodding her in the back if her speed slackened for even a second.

Finally they reached the big man and Adella. Pushing Linn up against the chopper, her captor spoke rapidly and furiously in Spanish to his companions. His tirade was answered by low laughter from the woman and a guffaw from the big man.

Linn turned her head and tried to see the big man's face but both he and the woman stood in the shadows. The rough, loud laugh still sounded vaguely familiar. *Was that why the man had not spoken before? Was he afraid I might recognize his voice?*

Linn tried to examine her arms and knees in the moonlight. Her right arm throbbed like a bad toothache and her right knee had a cut from which blood was trickling down her leg. *I guess I should be thankful I'm not hurt any worse,* she thought.

After a brief conference with the other two, the small Mexican man spoke to Linn. "Geet in the chopper," he ordered.

"Where are you taking me?" Linn asked without moving.

"Do what I tell you!"

Feeling helpless and realizing she had no choice, Linn climbed into the helicopter and sat down. The wiry Mexican sprang up behind her. Linn saw the woman and man still standing in the shadows. They seemed to be waiting for something — or someone.

Suddenly a strong, acrid odor filled the cabin, and Linn turned in alarm to see where it was coming from. Without warning, a strong arm went around her neck. The next instant, the suffocating scent of chloroform filled her nostrils as a cloth covered her mouth and nose.

Linn fought wildly, trying not to breathe, but finally she could hold her breath no longer. She sucked in some air, gasped, and lost consciousness.

11

Penny had retired to her room after the late dinner. She was still deeply distressed over Bobby's disappearance. Linn had been understanding about Penny leaving the baby to call Bart but that had only made her feel worse.

Over and over she castigated herself. How could she have left Bobby alone when she knew the danger? She had let Bobby down. If she had not made that long call to Bart — breaking her promise to Linn — little Bobby would still be safe and snug in his bed.

What had gotten into her the past six months? Fighting with her mother and Linn and Jake.

Jake!

Jake was responsible for all of this! If he had not come into their lives, she would probably be at home with Bart as she should be! Without Jake's interference, she could have convinced her mother that Bart was right for her.

And the baby would still be okay, because Linn would have watched him more carefully than Penny had. But Jake had spoiled everything! Her face distorted with repugnance. *I despise him, and now he's coming down here to be a "bigshot" and run the show. Well, let him! Maybe when he makes a complete fool of himself, mother will come to her senses and send him packing!*

Suddenly, Penny realized she was very thirsty. She slipped a robe over her pajamas and went to the kitchen. On the way back, she noticed a tiny slit of light under Linn's door.

Linn must be having trouble sleeping, too, she decided. Knocking softly on the door, she listened, but there was no movement or sound. *Maybe Linn went to sleep with the light on,* she thought. She turned to go, and then noticed that the door was not fully closed. Her light tap had pushed it open a tiny bit.

A riffle of apprehension prickled Penny's scalp. *Maybe I'm getting paranoid,* she thought, *but it certainly won't hurt to see if Linn is all right.*

She gently pushed the door open and stuck her head in. "Linn! Linn, are you all right?" Then a quiver of fear began somewhere under her ribs. The bed was still neatly made-up. Penny moved into the room. It was empty.

With quick strides, she crossed the room and looked into the small nursery. A swift glance showed that it was empty also. Her heart began to thud. Turning back into the room, Penny considered. Could Linn have gone outdoors? Out on the *corredore* or into the garden?

I'll go out and see, she decided. Penny crossed to the door, then turned to once more sweep the room with her eyes. As they moved over the bed, she noticed something on the white bedspread.

Hurrying over, Penny saw that it was a folded sheet of paper. With an awful sinking feeling, Penny read the single line message twice.

I have gone out back to see a woman who has news of Bobby. Linn.

Maybe Linn is okay, she tried to reassure herself. *What should I do? If only I knew how long ago Linn wrote this note.*

Suddenly a voice spoke from the doorway behind her, and Penny started violently. Whirling around, she saw Alfred standing there, a glass of water in his hand.

"Is anything wrong?" he asked. "I came out for some water and saw Linn's door open."

"I hope not," Penny said worriedly. "That salty ham at dinner sent me to the kitchen for water, too, and I saw a light under Linn's door. When I came in, the room was empty. This was on her bed." She handed Alfred the note.

Alfred read the few words and handed it back. His dark eyes mirrored alarm. "Is that Linn's handwriting?"

"Yes," Penny said decisively, "but why would she go out of the house by herself at night? She would know it wasn't safe."

"It sounds like whoever wanted her to come outside, told her to come alone. Bobby would be her first concern and whoever it was promised her news of the baby.

"Let's go get Esteban before we go outside to see about her," Alfred suggested.

Esteban must not have been asleep either because he answered their knock at his door almost instantly. Penny and Alfred silently handed him the note.

Esteban rang a bell that brought Pablo — black hair rumpled and still buttoning his shirt — from a room in another part of the house. Questioning Penny hurriedly, Esteban found flashlights and the three men left through the back door. Penny, forced to remain behind, woke Alicia and Josie. After what seemed an eternity, the men returned to report there was no sign of Linn — or anyone else — anywhere around.

Esteban called the police, and this time two officers came quickly. They read the note, asked a few questions, and called the police station for more men. With their help, the whole area for several blocks around was searched. But no sign of Linn was found.

"It's just like when those kidnappers steal a baby," one officer said gloomily. "They vanish without a trace. It's like they never existed."

Penny felt her stomach knot with anxiety and despair. She, Penny, was to blame for this whole nightmare that was becoming more terrifying by the minute. She had left Bobby at the mercy of the kidnappers to pursue her own desires. Now Linn had left the protection of the house, desperate for news of her baby, and they had gotten her, too. And no one seemed to be able to do a thing!

She felt a hand on her shoulder and looked up to see Alfred's sympathetic brown eyes upon her. "Everyone is doing all they can to find them, Penny," he said gently. "The kidnappers are bound to slip up somewhere and then this thing will start unraveling."

"But it's all my fault!" Penny choked back a sob. "If only I hadn't left the baby alone!"

"Our hindsight is always better than our foresight," Alfred said. "It's a cliche, but very true anyway. You won't help the situation by beating yourself to death with guilt. We all need clear heads and lots of faith right now."

Penny looked up in surprise. "You believe in the Lord?"

Alfred chuckled. "Is that so strange? I started going to church with Josie and Eric a long time ago. The Lord has become a very special part of my life."

Penny searched Alfred's face. "He used to be in mine but-but I don't feel He's very pleased with me much of the time anymore."

"Why not?"

Penny hesitated and then said heatedly, "Because of Jake, mother's husband! I can't stand the man! And I know a Christian shouldn't feel that way. But he's — crude! I never thought mother would fall for a dumb rancher."

Alfred grinned and said teasingly, "And he took your mom away!"

A faint flush colored Penny's cheeks, and she said defensively, "Maybe partly, but that isn't all of it! We clashed from the first. He tries to boss me and run my life! It was his idea that I come out here away from 'Bart's influence' so I could 'think rationally' — those are his exact words — about my relationship with Bart. To see if I really loved him! And mother and Linn agreed that it was the very thing to do!"

"Why don't you pray about your family situation?" Alfred said seriously. "Even if God didn't see fit to change the situation, He could change the way you felt about it."

"I don't want Him to change the way I feel about Jake! I could never like him in a million years, and I don't want to! He runs Bart down and. . . ."

Alfred held up a placating hand. "Wait a minute — I didn't plan to meddle in your affairs. We do need to pray earnestly for the situation at hand."

"You don't want to hear about Bart, do you?" Penny demanded. "No one wants to hear about him! No one will let me explain how sweet he is or about his good points! All I hear is how he doesn't get a job, and the trouble he has been in. No one gives him a chance!"

Alfred's brown eyes were regarding Penny steadily as she finished. "What if the family were right," he said softly, "and they are only telling you because they love you and don't want to see you ruin your life?"

Penny's eyes became slits of green ice, and her voice brittled with scorn. "So, that's what you think, too! And you don't even know him! Thanks a lot for your sympathetic ear!"

"Any time," Alfred said, grinning affably.

Furious, Penny turned and stalked out of the room.

12

When Linn regained consciousness, she was disoriented and afraid. There was no light in the place she was lying, and strange scrabbling noises near at hand set her heart to pounding. She lay very still, trying to recall how she had come to this place.

Then she remembered. Bobby had been kidnapped. Luisa had come with a message, and Linn had followed her out of the house. Luisa had left her, and she had been taken in a car to an airport and chlorformed. No telling where she was now! *But I can't be very far from Veracruz,* she reasoned, *because I couldn't have been unconscious for a long time — or could I?*

That woman — Adella — had promised to take her to Bobby. Was it all just a trick to kidnap her, too? Were they planning to hold her as well as Bobby for ransom?

Her head throbbed till she could hardly

think. In fact, she seemed to hurt all over. Her right arm hurt the worst — a dull, pulsing ache. Her knees burned, and she recalled that both were skinned. She ran her fingers exploringly over them, and they stung worse. Down the side of her right leg, she felt a trail of dried blood.

Suddenly, something cold touched her arm, and she jerked violently away. There was the sound of little scurrying feet. *Rats! It must have been a rat's nose that touched me*, she thought in horror. Panic, like a giant wave, swelled inside Linn, threatening to engulf her.

Scrambling to her feet, Linn stared into the darkness. A faint light shone from a small window, high in a wall. She heard the sound of scurrying little feet again and drew back, bumping into a wall. She touched it, and her hand came away damp.

"Where am I?" she said aloud. The sound of her voice seemed to echo, like she was in a cave or underground room. Stamping her feet, she moved away from the wall, her hands held out in front of her. She heard another patter of little feet, and then all was quiet, except for a drip from somewhere near.

Again she stamped her feet, then began moving slowly along the uneven, stone floor, her hands still extended in front of her. Suddenly she touched something hard and wooden. Cautiously, she ran her hands over the object. It was a straight chair, rough to the touch, and splintery. Her exploring hands told her that the chair was obviously a discard, somewhat rickety, and had only three legs.

She heard a squeak and little feet upon the stone floor, and she banged the chair down. Silence once more filled the room except for the monotonous, annoying drip. Stooping, Linn touched the floor, recoiling from its damp, gritty feel. Steeling herself, she groped along the floor as far as her hands could reach and found two bricks. She laid them beside the broken chair and moved cautiously across the room. In just a few steps, she was at the opposite wall.

Slowly, she groped along the wall until she came to a corner. Then she walked carefully across to the other wall, tripping once on a brick. She picked up that brick, took two steps, and bumped into the other wall. Her place of incarceration was small, she decided, no more than ten by ten.

She moved back to the broken chair and laid her brick with the other two. "They'll do for weapons against the rats, and maybe against my captors, if I have an opportunity," she said aloud, comforted by the sound of her voice.

Peering around the room, Linn thought she saw an object in a corner not far from her. She moved toward it, stumbling over another brick which she collected. The object was a wooden box, a crate of some sort.

She carried it and the brick back to her little collection. Crouching down, she stacked the bricks one on top of the other and tried to use them for a fourth leg for the chair but they weren't high enough. Using the box, though, worked for a leg after she laid a brick on the top.

Moving the broken chair, the box, and all the bricks over to the corner nearest the dim, square window, Linn set the chair up again against the wall. She sat down in it gingerly. It seemed secure enough.

Leaving the chair, Linn felt her way around the room and discovered a door. She moved her hands over the door, coming away with a splinter in the process. Extracting the splinter from her finger with her teeth, she resumed her exploration more carefully. There was no door knob on her side, she found. She heaved her weight against the door, but it seemed as solid as the wall.

Linn went back to the makeshift chair.

Stacking her other bricks by its side, she sat down and drew her legs up to her chest. It wasn't comfortable, but at least she could lean her head against the damp wall at her side and have the other wall to help support the rickety chair.

And she could keep her feet off the floor away from the rats! Where had she read about rats chewing off fingers and toes of people in the ghettos? The gruesome thought sent shivers over her body.

Linn had not intended to sleep. But she began to pray aloud, softly, for Bobby's safety and for her own. She quoted the 23rd Psalm into the darkness of the room. Then the 91st Psalm. Many times before, this therapy had helped pull her through difficult situations. *What a joy it is to have God to talk to,* she thought. Peace began to seep into her spirit; her tense muscles relaxed, and she slept.

How long she slept, she didn't know. But suddenly she was awakened by a slight nip on her arm. She screamed and leaped to her feet. She heard a squeak, a small thud, and the scramble of little feet. Her eyes stared into the duskiness of her prison in horror as they picked up the figure of a large dark rat scurrying away. He obviously had climbed the box she had used for a chair leg.

Her heart beating erratically and her skin crawling with revulsion, Linn moved on trembly legs to stand under the small window. *It must be getting daylight,* she thought dully. The dirty window now admitted a ray of pale light.

Holding her arm up to the light, Linn saw with relief — and thankfulness — that the skin was barely pricked. One tiny drop of blood oozed out. She pressed the small nick until she squeezed out several drops of blood which she rubbed away with the hem of her skirt. If the rat was carrying a disease, surely the extra blood would wash it out.

The shaft of pale light — with dust motes capering down its length — revealed that her prison was indeed small, with a damp, dirt-encrusted floor. The walls of brick and mortar looked old and cracked in places. The room appeared to have been used for storage at one time. There were bits of grain and many rat and mice droppings.

Linn climbed back upon her perch on the chair, her legs drawn up. She shrank from even putting her feet upon the filthy floor any more than she had to. Her nostrils rebelled at the dank air reeking of rats and mildew.

Maybe now that it's daylight, the rats will go to bed, she thought hopefully.

The hours dragged on — two by her watch, but it seemed impossible that it was only two — and still no one came. She heard a rooster crow somewhere near and the bray of a donkey, but no human voice or steps approached. Several times she left her chair to walk about the room, stretching and exercising her cramped limbs.

She was also becoming very hungry and thirsty although she tried not to dwell on that. She thought longingly of the glazed ham, potatoes, and sweet rolls that she had scarcely touched the night before, and of the spicy salsa and green chili that she had already learned to enjoy. And a glass of that icy tea would be delectable!

Her thoughts were interrupted suddenly by the noise of heavy footsteps and the rattling of a chain. Someone was unlocking her door!

Springing down, Linn picked up a brick, which she hid behind her as she stood against the wall, waiting.

The door swung open and a big bulk stood in the doorway. The sudden, brilliant light from the door nearly blinded Linn, and she moved quickly to the side so she could see.

The man who stood in the door was not only tall, with bull-like neck and ham-like hands, but he also sported a big potbelly. His small beady eyes, set into a big-jowled, stubble-covered face, were watching her alertly. The thick lips parted in a sneer, revealing yellowed, gaped teeth.

"Remember me, Missus Randolph?"

"Yes — from last night," Linn said. The odor of strong tobacco, sweat, and leather filled her nostrils.

"Yeah — but from another time, too — maybe five years ago," the big man said, seemingly enjoying some huge, private joke.

Linn hesitated, her mind struggling to understand what he could mean. Then it hit her like a huge fist in her stomach! This man was one of the Mayan artifact smugglers she had encountered five years ago at Moonshell, the mansion near Corpus Christi where the Randolphs had vacationed.

"I see yeer rememberin'," the burly man laughed.

"Carlos Zorro," Linn said slowly. "You're one of his men."

"Frank Oliver at cha service," the man said mockingly with a little bow. "Now that the interductions is over, ya better come wit me. The lady wants to see ya. And put down the brick, it won't do ya no good. I

102

could flatten ya with one little blow, if I needed to." His evil-looking eyes held no mirth now.

Stunned, Linn dropped the brick and meekly followed him out the door.

13

Linn stood in the brilliance of the sun and shaded her eyes. *The sun seems brighter here than any place else in the world,* she thought. Looking about her, she saw that she was at the end of the main street of a small village. The room from which she had emerged was, indeed, built under a small hill.

After observing the one and two room adobe houses strung along the cobbled street, tiled roofs interspersed with thatched roofs, she decided her prison actually might have been someone's living quarters at one time.

"This way," Frank said brusquely.

The way he indicated was a path that led toward a gate in a high wall. Beyond the stone wall, green trees waved in the breeze. The upper story and high dome of a huge hacienda rose, splendid and elegant.

Frank hurried her up the path, through

the gate, and into a courtyard. Grabbing her arm, he drew her rapidly across the courtyard and around the huge building along a flagstone pavement as if he didn't want anyone to see her. As he rushed her along, she glimpsed gorgeous beds and pots of gardenias, camellias, flame vines, roses, and many other varieties of plants as well as vines, shrubs, and trees.

They were approaching the back entrance to the mansion — a high, massive door of oak and brass. It looked old and weathered but sturdy and somewhat formidable. Carved into the door were two skillfully wrought figures of foxes, one seated and the other standing, as if on guard. Linn's heart quickened in hope and fear.

Frank lifted the knocker and dropped it quickly three times. The door was opened immediately by a swarthy, muscular young man with a heavy mustache. Frank spoke a few words in Spanish, and the man motioned them inside.

He led them down a short hall, up a spiraling stairway, and down another short hall. Pausing, the young man tapped softly. The door was opened by a slender *criada* dressed in a simple white cotton dress. But the simplicity of her frock only accented the creaminess of her complexion, her luminous brown eyes framed in long dark eyelashes, and full, rose-tinted lips.

A voice called from behind the maid, "Margarita, is that *Senora* Randolph? If so, bring her in."

Linn recognized the throaty voice of the driver of the car who had abducted her the night before.

The maid spoke in a softly accented voice, "Come in."

Luxurious, beautiful, sumptuous were not strong enough words to describe the spacious room Linn stepped into. Pale green carpet, resilient and lush, was underfoot. Mirrors, polished mesquite furnishings, hanging plants, plush sofas and pillows all spoke of taste and money. One complete wall was of glass, with double doors leading onto a gallery. Beyond, Linn could see the tops of trees and a mass of gorgeous bougainvillea under a magnificent dome.

She stood entranced just inside the door, drinking in the splendor and beauty of the room, until a soft, cultured voice spoke her name.

"Mrs. Randolph, how delightful to have you at Guarida de los Zorros, or perhaps I should translate. Welcome to The Foxes' Lair." The throaty voice was mocking. "I trust you had a pleasant sleep."

Linn turned. A delicately built, elegant blonde stood before her. Her hair was swept up into a mass of curls; long dark lashes and finely arched dark brows set off her dark blue eyes. Her parted lips showed perfect white teeth, except for one lower one which showed a faint glimmer of gold at its upper edge.

This must be Adella. She's beautiful, Linn thought.

Then Adella turned her head to speak to the maid, and Linn almost gasped out loud. On the left side of the well-shaped head a berry-red stain spread from the corner of her eye almost to the line of honey-blonde hair, a cruel mockery of the woman's exquisite beauty.

"Margarita, you and Frank may go now," she said. Nodding, Frank backed out the door and the slender *criada* slipped quietly away through another door after a softly murmured, *"Si, Senora."*

Adella turned back toward Linn. "This is *Senora* Zorro's suite. Come with me."

Linn followed Adella through an open doorway into what was obviously an office, although exquisitely furnished. Adella waved Linn to a cushioned leather armchair and moved to take the chair behind a large, neat desk.

For a full moment Adella looked at Linn with a probing, speculative stare. Finally, Linn broke the silence that was quickly becoming unnerving. "What have you done with my baby? You promised to take me to him."

"That I did and I will. But first we must have a short talk. My name is Adella Fernandez, and I am the secretary of *Senora* Bonnie Leeds de Zorro. An old friend of yours, I understand." The words and eyes were once more mocking.

"So Bonnie is the person behind the kidnapping of my baby and myself?" Linn said. "I should have known!"

The arched brows lifted "I didn't say that *Senora* Zorro knows nothing of the abduction of yourself or your baby. Carlos Zorro, her husband, is the one who planned all this — as a surprise for Bonnie. He embarked on the lucrative business of kidnapping and selling pretty Mexican peasant babies to wealthy, childless couples. And then, when he heard you were in Mexico with your son, he came up with a beautiful plan."

"Where is Bonnie?" Linn interrupted.

"She's in the United States for a few months," Adella said. "Her husband, *Senor* Zorro, had to be away for awhile on business, so she decided to spend the time in the

States, taking care of some business of her own."

Adella smiled. "Those two are so much in love. Theirs is the storybook kind of romance that one seldom sees anymore. *Senor* Zorro is always trying to think of new ways to please her. When he came up with this idea to kidnap *your* baby and sell him, he knew she would be pleased. He knew how much Bonnie hates you for something she said you did to her in the past. And the *Senor* himself owes you a debt for almost sending him to prison five years ago."

Linn felt her heart leap with horror, and her throat constricted painfully. "S-surely he wouldn't s-sell my baby! That's diabolical!"

"Yes, isn't it," Adella said, smiling slowly.

She's enjoying this, Linn thought in bewilderment. *Why? Certainly I have never done anything to this woman; she is a stranger to me.*

"But Carlos must know he can never get away with this!" Linn heard her voice rise but seemed unable to control it.

"Why not?" Adella said nonchalantly. "He has stolen a dozen or more peon babies and sold them. Your baby is no better than theirs. And the stupid police have no hint of who the kidnappers are! Certainly they would not suspect the aristocratic Zorro family!" she finished triumphantly.

"Why would you help to steal babies? Don't you have any feeling for the pain and suffering you are putting the parents through?"

Adella laughed callously. "All the babies but yours are from very poor Mexican parents who can barely feed themselves, let alone children. The babies are really much better off in their new homes. They'll have good educations and plenty of everything — including love."

"But the peasants love their babies just as much as anyone else!" Linn exclaimed vehemently.

"My, my! Listen to the champion of the poor," Adella mocked. "You don't know the first thing about poverty, not the grinding, demeaning poverty that many of the poor of Mexico know!"

"Perhaps not," Linn said impatiently, "but that doesn't change the truth of what I said. And may I see my baby now? You said he was here."

"Oh, you shall see him!" Adella responded. "In fact, you will be allowed to care for him for the next week. You will even have a personal maid to assist you." She laughed cruelly. "You have exactly seven days with your baby! Then he will be taken from your arms, and you will never see him again!"

Linn's face went white and her voice trembled, "Where are you taking him?"

"He has already been sold to a family out of the country. You will never know who he was sold to or even in what country he is."

Adella laughed her low, husky laugh. "You will be released — unharmed as I promised — and you will go home and live the rest of your life sorrowing for your son!"

Linn did not know tears were running down her cheeks as she stared mutely at Adella. Horror rendered her speechless until Adella spoke again mockingly. "Those tears will be only the first of many. I think *Senor* Zorro has come up with the ultimate plan for revenge. Don't you agree?"

Linn sprang forward and gripped Adella by the arms. Her voice shook. "I won't let you do this! It's cruel and evil and—"

Adella tried to pull away, but Linn tightened her grip, "Give me my baby!"

Adella called out a single word in Spanish and instantly a tall, muscular woman moved from behind a colorful screen nearby. Adella spoke a few rapid words which Linn could not understand, and the woman laid large rough hands on Linn's wrists and squeezed. Linn winced with pain and released her hold upon Adella.

Adella stepped back and chuckled. "Meet

111

your maid, Francesca. She will help you with the baby during the day and care for your needs as well. But she is also your guard, by day — and by night. She is very loyal to me. Francesca understands Spanish, but unfortunately she cannot speak, so she won't be much company."

She turned away, "Come, we will take you to your son."

Speechless, Linn followed her, the lumbering maid almost trodding on her heels. Her thoughts were in a turmoil. Surely this could not be happening! How could anyone do the wicked thing that Carlos had planned for her and Bobby? How could she bear to lose Bobby — never to see him again, never to hold him or hear his happy chuckle! A cry filled her heart. *Dear God, please don't let them take away my baby!*

They passed into a gallery that overlooked the patio. As they followed the parapet, Linn looked down and saw a dolphin fountain, water spouting from its mouth; brightly colored flowers filled beds and large clay pots of many shapes and color. A coconut tree and two citrus trees thrust their heads up toward the sunlight flooding into the atrium through the glass dome.

Adella paused at a door and tapped three times. A smiling *criada* opened the door and stepped back for them to enter. Linn's glance quickly swept the room. It was a large, well-furnished bedroom. But Linn was not interested in how the room was furnished. In the corner was a baby bed!

Linn heard a happy gurgle and in a few quick strides was at its side. Bobby was lying there, clean and safe, kicking his chubby legs and waving his arms happily.

When he saw her leaning over him, his eyes grew wide, and happy sounds burst from his soft baby lips. His legs churned and his arms waved with almost frantic delight when she bent and took him into her arms. Chortling aloud, he planted a wet kiss on her face.

For a long moment Linn forgot about the others in the room and the precariousness of her situation as she hugged Bobby to her fiercely, glorying in the feel of his soft arms about her neck. Her heart lifted in a prayer of thankfulness to God. Whatever lay ahead, at least for the present she had her baby in her arms.

She raised her eyes and saw Adella standing at the foot of the crib watching her. Shock thrust between her ribs like a keen knife, causing Linn to almost gasp aloud. Adella's eyes were flaming cauldrons of naked hate, and her lips were twisted in undisguised loathing.

Then, abruptly, Adella's face and eyes changed. Her lips curved into a smile, and her eyes glowed with warmth. The change was so abrupt that Linn wondered if she had imagined the malice in Adella's face.

Adella moved away and for a second Linn closed her eyes. In her mind's eye, she saw Adella's face again, twisted with hate and vengefulness. No, she had not been mistaken! *But why,* her mind shrieked, *why does Adella hate me — and possibly Bobby? What have I ever done to Adella? She's a complete stranger!*

Still holding Bobby, Linn followed Adella and strove to speak calmly over the turmoil churning in her mind. "Adella, why do you seem to take pleasure in what Carlos is planning? You seem to — to hate me. Why?"

Adella did not turn her head but stood looking out the large picture window that framed the gallery and the patio-garden. For a moment she didn't answer, and then she laughed softly, low and throaty. "Why shouldn't I despise you? I'm a loyal employee, and you hurt both *Senor* and *Senora* Zorro."

"For goodness sakes," Linn said in exasperation, "that was a long time ago! Bonnie imagined I took Clay away from her, but when I met him, I didn't even know Bonnie existed or that he was engaged to anyone!"

"And after you two broke up, *Senora* Zorro again was to marry the one she loved, and you again broke it up!" Adella said with asperity.

"I was still married to Clay," Linn ejaculated. "So I certainly did not take away Bonnie's beloved. He was *my* husband!"

Dislike gleamed in Adella's dark blue eyes, now fixed upon Linn. "But you did try to send Carlos and Bonnie to prison five years ago. You can't deny that!"

"They were the ones who drew me into their smuggling game," Linn said. "I did not ask to have any part in it. They broke the law and should have had to pay the consequences."

Adella's laugh rang out. "But they didn't! Money and influence are great things! I expect you have been very angry that they got off scott free?"

Linn's anger suddenly vanished, and she spoke quietly, "No, I am not angry that Bonnie and Carlos did not go to prison. But I would like to see them drop this foolish idea of revenge against Clay and me. Is that love? Believe me, we have never meant to hurt Bonnie — or Carlos."

A strange look flashed over Adella's face, and then she shrugged. "Well, you don't have to convince me. I only follow orders. And Carlos has ordered your baby sold — and you released unharmed. So that is what will take place!"

Her lovely face took on a sly look. "By the way, Carlos will receive twenty-five thousand dollars for Bobby. You should be pleased. That's five thousand more than he gets for the most endowed Mexican baby."

Linn felt a wave of nausea wash over her. "I want to talk to Carlos," she said. "Clay and I will pay him more than twenty-five thousand." Her voice took on a pleading note. "Please, let me talk to Carlos — or even to Bonnie!"

Adella looked at her solemnly from fathomless blue eyes. Then threw back her head and laughed. Abruptly, she broke off the laughter and walked from the room without another word. Linn heard the click of the lock as the door closed. Then another burst of laughter rang out as Adella's heels clicked away down the gallery.

14

Penny was angry.

It had been two days since Bobby's and Linn's disappearance. Her mother, Kate, and her mother's husband, Jake Stone, had arrived the evening before. To Penny's chagrin, Jake had immediately begun to question everyone in the household; had gone to the police station and talked to the police twice today, and now he was grilling each servant individually again.

Senor Molinas and his wife didn't seem to be taking offense, but Penny was embarrassed. She had just come from her mother's room where she had urged Kate to insist that Jake let the police handle the case. But her mother had sided with Jake — calmly and sweetly — but still she had taken Jake's side.

"Penny," she had said, "Jake is just doing what he can to help. The police have not uncovered even a single clue, so if Jake can come up with just one little overlooked *something* for the police to work on, it would help. After all, the police can't put all their efforts on this case and Jake can."

"Clay is coming in tomorrow, so then he can take over," Penny had said.

Kate had looked at Penny with troubled eyes. "Penny, this is not a case of any one person 'running things.' We are all just doing what we can to get Linn and Bobby back."

"I wish you would tell that to Jake," Penny muttered as she left the room. "He doesn't act like anyone else but him is capable of doing anything!"

Penny was now standing in the patio-garden, absently watching the goldfish drift among the water plants. Their leisurely movements slowly began to transmit a feeling of calm to her spirit.

If only things were like they used to be, she thought. Then there had just been her and her mother and Clay and Linn. No, she decided, she wouldn't wish for that. She would not wish for darling little Pamela — Penny's shadow and adorer — or sweet little Bobby to be excluded from the family group. But she could surely do without Jake! *He* was the one who had ruined everything!

Suddenly a voice spoke almost at her

elbow, and Penny started.

"Sorry, I spooked you," Jake said in his overly loud voice.

Jake plunked down his large frame in a small, ornately curved chair, and Penny winced. *If it wasn't for ruining the Molinas's chair, it would do me good to see that fragile chair break and spill him out on the ground,* she thought maliciously.

"You know, girl," Jake said musingly, "I think that maid, Luisa, is hiding something. If only I could get her to talk!"

Penny spoke stiffly as she began to edge away. The last person in the world she wanted to talk to right now was her mother's husband. "What makes you think that? Luisa just lost a baby to the kidnappers, too."

"I know," Jake said, his bright blue eyes kindling with excitement. "Don't you think she is a little *too* unconcerned about losing that baby?"

He had captured Penny's attention now — and disdain. "Of course she's concerned," Penny cried. "When he was first kidnapped, she cried and wailed like a poor lost soul!"

"Sure, I know she did at first. That's what everyone tells me. But now she can talk about it and doesn't even let out a sniffle. Is it natural to get over losin' a baby that quick? I ask you, is that natural?"

"How should I know?" Penny retorted. *Who was he to be judging Luisa? Maybe she had to pretend she hadn't lost a baby in order to cope with the situation.* Penny did not quite dare to voice her thoughts aloud, but they obviously showed on her expressive face.

"You don't have to get your fur all bent the wrong way," Jake growled. "*Someone* knows somethin' about this kidnapping business, and I aim to find out what!"

Penny spun about, her eyes sparking fire. "Jake, the Molinas won't like it if you keep harassing their servants."

Jake looked at her with calm blue eyes. "I can't help what they don't like! I'm not stopping till I get to the bottom of this business." He turned abruptly and strode off toward the kitchen.

Penny groaned and ground her teeth. "Stupid, pig-headed old goat!" she muttered.

"Oh, I don't know about that," a bantering voice said. Alfred stood nearby; his dark eyes glinted with amusement behind their horn-rimmed glasses. His thin lips were twisted into a crooked grin.

Penny turned her back on him rudely, but Alfred continued in that infuriating tone,

"You know, there isn't anyone who is working harder at finding Linn and Bobby than Jake. At least give him an E for effort."

Penny turned back around and skewered him with angry eyes. "It makes him feel like a big shot to go around acting like a Perry Mason!"

"Maybe Perry Mason is who we need," Alfred said calmly. Suddenly Alfred's eyes and lips were no longer smiling. "Penny," he said gently, "why don't you give up this grudge and give Jake a break. You might grow to like him."

"Stay out of my affairs, Alfred Benholt!" Penny snarled.

Alfred stood still, regarding her with something that looked strangely like pity.

Penny felt tears sting her eyes — tears of anger, tears of frustration, and other undefinable, mixed-up feelings. She ducked her head and turned away.

She felt a touch on her arm. Alfred was standing very near her, looking down at her. His voice was soft. "Penny, it hurts me to see what is happening to you. This anger and hatefulness is so unlike what I remember of you. Hate and resentment will only destroy you. Let them go!"

"What do you care?" Penny said spitefully. She dashed the tears from her eyes with a slightly unsteady hand and started to walk away.

Alfred moved quickly to stand in front of her. His voice was husky and soft. "I do care, Penny — very, very much. Because I care for you — very, very much."

Tears were again clouding Penny's vision. She had no idea why, and it made her furious. Shaking her head, she ran toward the house.

She was restlessly prowling about her room a few minutes later when she heard a tap on her door and her mother's voice.

"Come in," she called. *Why did mother have to come right now?* she thought. *I just don't want to talk to anyone — except for Bart. And thanks to Jake's interference, I'm a long way from him!* But she tried to act gracious as her mother sat down.

It seemed like an eternity ago that the little chats she and her mother had had were a source of pleasure for both of them. But not any more — thanks to big Jake Stone!

Kate curled her slim figure up in a large armchair, like a girl. Her slightly faded green eyes — so like Linn's and Penny's — held worry and a shadow of apprehension.

Penny seated herself in a small rocker and waited. *I hope she isn't going to lecture me,* she thought. *I'm just not in the mood!*

"Penny, I want to tell you something about Bart. I had hesitated to tell you this, but feel I must."

Penny's eyes narrowed. *I might have known,* she thought. *I wish everyone would let us alone and let us live our own lives.* With great effort, she remained silent.

"Jake gave Bart a job on the ranch."

"I know, Bart told me," Penny inserted quickly. "He didn't take it because he feels he isn't suited for that."

A strange look crossed Kate's face. "So that's what he told you?"

"What do you mean? So that's what he told me?" Penny demanded testily.

Kate sighed. "Penny, have you ever wondered why you are always on the defensive about Bart? We're only thinking of what's best for you."

"Everyone meddles in my affairs under the guise of doing what's best for me," Penny said bitterly.

Anger sprang into Kate's eyes, and her gentle lips firmed into a straight line. For a moment she didn't speak. When she did, her voice was unemotional. "Bart worked for Jake only a few days. He was late every day, and the last day he showed up for work, he was in no condition to work."

Concern jumped into Penny's eyes. "What

was wrong with him?"

"He was so stoned that he could scarcely talk. He passed out on the job. Jake searched his pockets and found cocaine — and marijuana. Jake took him home, and his mother refused to believe her son had passed out from drugs. She took him to the emergency room at the hospital, and the doctor there confirmed it. But she still will not accept it."

"How do you know what the doctor said?" Penny demanded. She was visibly shaken but still defiant.

"Jake carried him into the emergency room and stayed until he heard the verdict," Kate said.

"So Jake fired him!" Penny stated angrily.

"No, Penny," Kate said, "his mother called the next day and said the work was too hard for Bart, and he wouldn't be back."

Penny felt cold and hot, and then a trembling seemed to start somewhere deep inside. Bart couldn't still be using drugs! He had promised her he would never touch them again! She just couldn't believe it was possible. Bart wouldn't lie to her, and he had said he didn't take the job.

Then a thought came to her, and she spoke it almost before it was birthed. "You only have Jake's word for all of this. How do

I know he is telling the truth?"

Kate looked shocked. "Of course he is telling the truth! What a thing to say!"

"Bart's mother doesn't think Bart was using drugs — and I don't either! None of you like him, so you always think the worst of him!"

Sparks of anger flared in Kate's green eyes. "Penny, you are a big girl now, use your head! I'll admit Bart is charming and good-looking, but he *is* using drugs. It's time you accept facts before you wind up with a drug addict for a husband."

"So, now he is not just dabbling in drugs, he's a drug addict! See! You always think the worst of him! Well, I think the worst of Jake Stone. I think he gave Bart a job so he could frame him and make me think he is using drugs again."

Kate was obviously having difficulty holding her temper, but she spoke quietly. "You said Bart told you he didn't accept the job. If he lied about that, he could be lying about the drugs, too."

"Did you see Bart working on the ranch?" Penny pressed. Jake had a house at the edge of town, and Penny knew the ranch was a couple of miles from town.

"No," Kate admitted, "I didn't personally see Bart at the ranch, but I believe Jake."

"And I believe Bart," Penny said triumphantly.

The anger had gone from Kate's face, replaced by weary resignation. "Very well, young lady, believe what you wish."

As she walked to the door, Penny noticed that her mother was beginning to look old. Alarm sprang up in her heart, but she quickly stifled it. She mustn't let sympathy for her mother influence her right now. She loved Bart, and she meant to marry him! And her mother would do anything in her power to keep her from that.

But a little nagging doubt brushed her thoughts. What if the family were right and she was wrong? It would be a nightmare being married to a drug addict. But she thrust the thought away. A picture of Bart's curly head and crooked grin rose in her mind. She could almost hear his husky voice whispering in her ear! Bart loved her and that was all that mattered!

15

Linn was desperately homesick and lonely. It was now the evening of the fourth day since she had been abducted. The maid had just taken Bobby away for the night.

She was thankful to have her baby with her all day, and treasured each hour with him, but every evening the shy, silent little nurse came and took him away. *Perhaps Adella thinks I might try to escape with him when everyone is asleep,* Linn thought. *She knows I won't if my baby is somewhere else in the mansion. But I can be thankful for one thing! Pamela was not with me on this trip so Adella didn't get her clutches on her!*

Linn went into the bathroom to brush and floss her teeth in preparation for the night. Then she brushed her hair two hundred strokes with the expensive hairbrush on her dressing table. She had never brushed her hair so much in her life! In her boredom, it seemed she had to invent things to do or go stir-crazy.

Linn missed Clay and Pamela dreadfully. She saw no one during the long days except her guard, Francesca; Adella's pretty personal maid, Margarita, who brought their food; and the *criada* who came for Bobby each evening at seven.

Linn had tried to talk with the maid who cared for her son at night, but she had shaken her head emphatically. She either could not or would not speak English. Margarita smiled at her, but always left the food and departed quickly, refusing to speak also.

Linn was torn between wishing for the long days to end and the feeling that somehow she must stop them from ending because then her son would be taken away forever. She had to remind herself constantly that God could prevent that from happening and that He was still in control.

Adella had been in each day, very briefly, usually with taunting, malicious words.

"Put his picture in your mind vividly," she had said today, "for you have only three more days to cuddle him and care for him. I know his new mama is aching to get her hands on him."

Adella laughed her low, husky laugh.

"Can you imagine that he may not even learn to speak English? Poor, little Randolph heir, not even to know the language of his natural parents."

Linn had a terrible urge to throttle Adella's graceful neck. But Francesca stood almost at her elbow. Choking down angry words, she turned back to her baby and gathered him to her with such fierceness that he wriggled in alarm.

She had to pray almost constantly to keep hatred from taking possession of her mind. Hate for vengeful Bonnie, for the lawless Carlos, and for sadistic Adella, their willing, even eager, accomplice.

Linn was not allowed to leave her room except for a few brisk turns around the gallery each night. Francesca was always in attendance and it was only after darkness had fallen and Bobby had been carried away. The doors into the hall and the gallery were locked when she retired.

"Remember, Francesca sleeps just outside your door," Adella had warned her, "and she's a light sleeper. If you should try to escape, and I wasn't here, she might forget her own strength and hurt you. And I don't want that to happen. Especially your early demise! Carlos wishes you to have a long life to mourn your son!"

Linn turned out all the lights except for a small desk light and stretched out on her bed. It was only seven-thirty, but Francesca had gone, and all was very quiet.

Why does Adella take such a sadistic pleasure in my trouble? she pondered. The thought kept recurring that perhaps the woman was really Bonnie. She summoned Adella's image to her mind just as she had done many times during the past four days.

Adella had honey-blonde hair and blue eyes. Bonnie had black hair and dark brown eyes. She thought carefully. The hair could be a wig, of course, and she had heard there were now contact lenses that could change the color of one's eyes.

And Adella's voice was different, husky and throaty. But Bonnie was always a good actress who delighted in casting herself in many roles, she recalled. She could change from one role to the other with lightning speed. Perhaps she had practiced a different voice until she could do it with ease.

But what of the dark red birthmark? Bonnie had no such defect. The berry-red stain on Adella's face was partially concealed by skillfully applied make-up but not completely erased. Could the birthmark be painted on, as a disguise? It was a possibility, even though it appeared to be genuine.

Disguising herself as someone else to deceive Linn and the others of the household would be something that would appeal to Bonnie. She delighted in theatrics! *If only I could talk to some of the servants here,* she thought. But Adella wasn't allowing that. Even Margarita, who could speak both English and Spanish, was plainly not allowed to talk to her.

There must be other people here at Quarida de los Zorros, Linn thought. *What about Carlos's mother, Carlota? Didn't she live here?*

Her heart quickened. *Perhaps that's why I'm being held so secretly,* she thought. *Maybe Carlota is here. If I could only get free and talk to her! Maybe she knows nothing of Carlos's plot! Alicia had said once that Carlota was from a fine, respectable family. If only I could get free!*

But she had tried both doors before and every window; all were securely locked. And she wasn't sure where Francesca slept, by her door in the hall or by the one that led onto the gallery.

She got up and began to pace the floor. Her helplessness was so frustrating! Carlos and Adella had planned and carried everything out with seemingly no flaw.

"Dear God, please help me — and Bobby," she whispered. "You are our only hope. And please, comfort and help Clay and Penny during this time. Clay almost surely knows of our disappearance by now and he will be frantic."

Anger suddenly surged into her heart as she thought of Penny. If her sister had not become so obstinate and self-centered that all she thought about was herself and that wild Bart Youngblood, neither Linn nor her baby would be in the ruthless hands of Adella Fernandez and Carlos Zorro.

But the pathetic image of Penny after the kidnapping sprang into Linn's mind, dissipating her anger. She knew the agony Penny must be feeling now! One other thing Linn knew with certainty: In spite of Penny's perverseness of late, she still loved Linn — and Bobby — very deeply.

Linn looked at her watch. It was eight-thirty. She might as well go to bed. There was nothing to do, not even anything to read. There were only two books in the room — placed there purposely by Adella, Linn was sure. Both were written in English, and both were horror stories of atrocities committed during World War II, complete with pictures, many of them of children. She had placed the two books in a drawer, out of sight.

Linn showered and slipped into a clean nightgown. Adella must have planned this for some time because there were clothes in the drawers and closets which fit Linn. Not fancy or expensive but plenty to meet her needs. A new toothbrush, toothpaste, deodorant, and other toiletries showed preparation. And Bobby was also well supplied with clothes that fit. This was no spur-of-the-moment kidnapping.

But Linn and Clay had planned this trip only a couple of months ago. How had Carlos and Adella known of their plans? Linn climbed into bed as she thought of this. *Someone must have been keeping close track of our activities to know our plans,* Linn thought. To know that the whole family had been closely watched was not a comforting thought.

For quite a while Linn lay in bed praying and quoting Scriptures in her mind. How she missed her Bible! She had asked for one, but Adella had given her a contemptuous look and not even bothered to answer her.

Suddenly Linn became aware of a strange sound. Her heart began to pound and she cocked her head, trying to pinpoint the source of the faint sound. It was very near and sounded like a sliding door rolling on a smoothly oiled track. The sound stopped. Linn switched on the light and looked around the room with frightened eyes. Everything was in place.

Perhaps a room next door is occupied, she thought. But this was the first time she had heard any sound during the night. Her portion of the house seemed completely unoccupied. It had given her a lonely, desolate feeling.

She heard a sound again. It sounded like muffled footsteps, but the sound faded out almost at once.

It shouldn't be strange if someone is occupying the next room, she thought. *Perhaps Francesca decided to sleep there instead of outside my door. I'm just getting jumpy,* Linn decided as she lay back down. But her nerves remained taut, and her ears strained to hear even though she willed them not to.

When there was no further sound, she finally began to relax. She was drifting into slumber when the rolling sound came again. Instantly she was wide awake, every nerve tingling. She had left a tiny nightlight on, but it gave very little light. Her eyes darted about the room. At first she saw nothing, and then she gasped. There was a black, yawning gap about three feet wide in the wall to her right!

As Linn groped wildly for the light switch, a dark-shrouded figure glided swiftly from the opening and across the room to the bed. Linn threw off her sheet and was out of the bed on the opposite side from the figure with the speed of a striking rattlesnake. She leaped to switch on the light.

Margarita, Adella's personal maid, stood by the bed, her dark eyes blinking in the bright glare as the light came on. A dark cloth was drawn about her face and shoulders.

"What do you want, sneaking in here like this?" Linn demanded. "You nearly scared me to death!"

Fear shone in Margarita's eyes, and she put a slim finger to her lips as she breathed a faint, "Shhhhh."

Suddenly the lock on Linn's door rattled. Margarita again breathed a quick "shhhh" and dashed across the carpeted room to the opening in the wall. The wall had barely closed together when Francesca slammed into the room.

Her glittering black eyes raked the room, and then came to rest upon Linn, still standing near the light switch. Linn tried to act nonchalant. She turned and walked to the bathroom door on extremely shaky legs.

Francesca crossed the room swiftly, rudely pushed Linn aside, and looked into the bathroom, even drawing aside the shower curtain to peer into the tub enclosure. When she moved out, Linn went inside and ran water in the basin, leisurely washing her face. She could hear Francesca banging about the room, checking the closets.

When Linn re-entered her bedroom, Francesca was looking under Linn's bed. She checked all the windows and the other door while Linn watched. Linn's heart was beating like a tom-tom, but she tried to speak calmly, "There's no one here but me. I am somewhat restless, and since you are here, I could surely use a glass of milk."

The big woman frowned and once more let her eyes travel over the whole of the room. When Linn asked again for some milk, the gargantuan Mexican woman simply glared at her and stalked from the room.

Adella had said Francesca could understand only Spanish, but Linn was not sure this was true. However, she received no milk and saw no more of her guard or her clandestine visitor. Linn stayed awake for several hours, hoping Margarita would return through the secret panel in the wall. But it remained closed. She wondered if Margarita was friend or enemy. At this point, Linn preferred anyone to her known foes in this den of foxes.

16

Linn awoke the next morning to the gentle touch of Bobby's night nurse. Until this morning, Linn was always up, dressed and waiting when the little maid brought Bobby to her. This morning she had overslept, having tossed and turned until nearly four o'clock.

A few minutes later, with Francesca right behind her, Margarita brought in breakfast for Linn, Francesca, and Bobby. There was one thing for which Linn could not fault Adella: good, well-prepared meals were always provided.

Linn was also thankful that Francesca always loaded a plate for herself and ate at a small table near the window, leaving a larger table for Linn and Bobby. With a kiss on his soft dimpled cheek, Linn lifted Bobby into his highchair and added a little soft scrambled egg to his baby cereal. When she unfolded the terrycloth bib that always accompanied each meal, Linn noticed a piece of paper in the little pocket at the bottom. Was it a note for her? She glanced at Francesca. The big woman seemed to be totally absorbed in her breakfast.

Carefully, Linn drew out the paper but before she could hide it, Francesca's big hand closed around Linn's slender one. With a dreadful sinking feeling in the pit of her stomach, Linn surrendered the paper, a piece of children's construction paper.

Francesca opened it, stared at it for a moment, and then dropped the paper back on the table with a disgusted grunt. Linn picked it up, and disappointment smacked her in the face. A big yellow moon with a smiling face stared at her from the sheet. There was nothing else on it.

"Just a picture for you," she told Bobby as she held it up for him to see. He grabbed for it with a plump fist, and she drew it back. "No, no, Bobby, you're supposed to look at it, not eat it."

Dropping it back on the table, she began to spoon cereal into Bobby's eager mouth. When the meal was finished, Linn found a thumbtack in a desk drawer and put the moon picture up on the wall above Bobby's bed. She supposed someone in the kitchen had drawn it for Bobby, possibly Margarita.

Margarita! Surely if someone sent the picture she — or he — would know Bobby was too little to appreciate it. Could it be a message of some sort? Margarita had come to her room for some reason last night. *I'll study the picture more closely when Francesca leaves the room,* she decided.

It seemed like forever before Francesca left the room with their dishes. But as soon as the door clicked shut behind her, Linn dashed to the picture and took it down. Eagerly examining it from every angle and both sides, Linn's hopes soon dwindled. She could see no message, word, or even letter drawn on the paper. In extreme disappointment, she concluded that it was just a simple picture for Bobby. It was no more than a moon with a smiling face drawn on it.

Depression tried to settle upon her all morning. She tried to keep her mind on the promises of God, but her spirit felt like a mountain-sized hand of gloom was slowly squeezing hope from her.

At noon, when Margarita came with their lunch, Linn tried to engage her in conversation, but Margarita only smiled and shook her head Francesca hovered in the background; her glittering hawk-like eyes watched Margarita's every move. As

Margarita left the room, she paused for a second beside Bobby's crib where he was playing with a soft foam ball. She patted Bobby's fat cheek with her left hand.

Linn was standing at the end of the baby bed and to Margarita's right. As the pretty maid's hand came away from Bobby's cheek, she turned the palm toward Linn for an instant. A smiling moon face was drawn there. Linn carefully controlled any reaction. Unhurriedly, Margarita moved away and walked out the door as usual.

As Linn took the luncheon from the tray and placed it on the table, her mind was racing. What did Margarita mean by the smiling moon faces?

Then it struck her forcibly! Her heart began to beat so hard, she hoped eagle-eyed Francesca didn't notice. There was a message! Margarita was telling her she would be back tonight — so Linn would not be frightened as she had been the night before!

Linn prepared for bed early that night. Had she interpreted the message correctly or had there really been a message? She might be grasping at straws as her time with Bobby grew shorter. There were only two more days unless God gave her a miracle.

Linn did not plan to sleep, and for a long time she lay praying and quoting Scripture verses, softly but audibly.

In spite of her intentions, though, Linn was asleep when Margarita came. The first she knew of her presence was a softly whispered, "Please do not make a sound. Francesca has ears like a fox. Put on a robe and come quickly."

Linn was instantly awake. She had been afraid to leave her clothes on, lest Francesca come in and check on her. The woman could not only hear like a fox, she was also as cunning as one.

As a precautionary measure, Linn formed a blanket and pillow into the semblance of a human body under the sheet on the bed. Then Margarita grasped her arm, and the two slipped quickly into the dark gap in the wall. It slid smoothly back into place behind them.

Margarita flicked on a tiny penlight which faintly revealed a cramped, carpeted stairway leading downward into the darkness. "Careful, the steps are narrow," Margarita whispered. "Hold on to me."

The passageway was not wide enough for them to descend side by side, so Linn took a firm grip on Margarita's shoulder and carefully descended the stairs behind her.

Linn's mind churned with questions she could not ask. Was Margarita helping her escape? Her mind drew back from this. She would not leave without Bobby! She reached out and clutched the maid's arm. "Where are you taking me?"

Margarita only hissed at her softly to be quiet and moved off ahead of her again in the darkness. The steps were not only narrow, they made several abrupt turns before finally stopping at a blank wall. The slender maid felt along the wall, then Linn heard it roll back. They stepped through the small opening into a large, moonlit courtyard.

Linn instantly saw that it was not the one in the center of Adella and Bonnie's quarters. This was much larger, had more trees, and was not covered with a dome. Besides a brilliant silver moon, she saw stars blinking brightly overhead and felt a warm breeze brush her face and stir her hair.

"This is a different patio-garden," Linn whispered to Margarita.

"There are three large patios at Guarida de los Zorros," the young woman replied in her softly accented English. "This one is in the center and is the largest with the smaller ones on either end. The end ones are additions built onto the main house about twenty years ago. The kitchen, bakery, laundry, and servants quarters are on one end. The other is *Dona* Carlota's son's private wing. *Don* Carlos's patio is the only one with a dome over it. *Dona* Carlota likes the fresh, open air."

"Where are you taking me?" Linn asked again as Margarita took a step to move on.

"*Dona* Carlota wishes to speak with you. Come."

Margarita drew her along with a slender but strong hand. They crossed the patio on a winding stone walk and entered a wide, luxuriously furnished *corredore* dimly lighted by two shaded lamps. Margarita guided Linn swiftly across the loggia into a short hall and up a beautiful curving stairway with banisters of intricately fashioned wrought iron.

They came out onto a gallery overlooking the open patio. Wealth, beauty, and good taste showed on every side. Moving swiftly to a heavy carved door, Margarita spoke softly in Spanish. A woman's voice answered from inside. The maid opened the door and stood back for Linn to precede her.

The room Linn stepped into was a beautifully furnished sitting room. She only glimpsed the decor, however, as her eyes came to rest upon the lady who sat in a large, cushioned chair.

Although Linn could tell that *Dona* Carlota was quite old, she was still very beautiful. Small and fragile in appearance, she had fine, perfect features, and alert, velvety dark, glowing eyes. Her glossy black hair streaked with silver was draped with an exquisite black lace mantilla.

She rose to take Linn's hand, using a black cane to hold herself erect. A smile touched the thin, aristocratic lips. When she spoke, her English was perfect but delightfully accented; her voice was cultured and gracious.

"Welcome to Guarida de los Zorros. I am Carlota Rodriguez de Zorro. Please sit down. Would you like something to drink? Coffee or tea?"

Pressing the cool, petal-soft hand, Linn declined the drink and seated herself in a chair facing *Dona* Carlota. Margarita rushed to help settle her mistress back into her chair, then sat down on a leather-covered footstool a little to one side.

Carlota's dark eyes studied Linn briefly before she asked, "What are you doing at Guarida de los Zorros?"

Linn's heart gave a leap of hope. Did Carlos's mother not know of her son's blackmarket traffic in kidnapped babies? "My baby and I were abducted by your son's men and Adella," Linn said bluntly, "but we are not the only ones. At least a dozen babies have been kidnapped and sold thus far according to Adella."

Stunned amazement showed clearly in Carlota's eyes, and her hand fluttered to her chest as if she felt a twinge of pain there. Margarita jumped up, "Do you need your medicine, *Senora?*"

"No." Carlota waved her away with an impatient, frail hand. "It is nothing." Her dark eyes again sought Linn's. "This I cannot believe! Carlos has done things that were outside the law, I am grieved to admit. But to steal innocent babies and cause such sorrow! That I cannot believe!"

"But it is true!" Linn tried to stay calm, but it was difficult. This woman might be her only hope of freedom for Bobby and herself. She had to convince her that they were being held captive!

As she strove for the best words, Carlota spoke again. "You say my son kidnapped you and your baby. Why would Carlos kidnap you as well as the baby if he is really selling children, as you say? What would he want with you? He has a wife." Her brief smile was frosty. "And with his wealth, he could have all the extra ladies he desires without capturing a married, *Yanque* one."

"I know it sounds preposterous," Linn said, "but let me explain. Five years ago,

145

Carlos and Bonnie, your daughter-in-law, were involved with stolen artifacts. My husband and I were drawn into it also, though not willingly. According to Adella, Carlos feels I was to blame because they nearly went to jail. Also, Bonnie has carried a grudge against me for eight years because I married the man she had planned to marry. She swore to get even."

Carlota sat very still. Her gaze on Linn's face was unwavering and inscrutable.

Linn rushed on. "My sister Penny and I, and my six-month-old son, Bobby, are visiting friends in Veracruz. A week ago, a baby was kidnapped from a young couple who works for them. My baby was taken from the house a couple of days later, and then Adella lured me to her car with a promise of news about my son. When I went outside, Adella and two of Carlos's men kidnapped me and brought me here."

Carlota's voice was crisp and businesslike. "But I repeat. What does Carlos want with you?"

Linn's green eyes darkened with pain. "Adella tells me that Carlos came up with a plan to make me suffer, as revenge and also as a surprise to please Bonnie."

Linn swallowed hard. "She said I was to be allowed to care for my baby for seven

146

days. Then he was to be taken from my arms, and I would never see him again. He has already been-been s-sold to adoptive parents in another country, according to Adella."

Carlota suddenly laughed, a tinkle of haughty disdain. "Do you expect me to believe such a fairy tale? In the first place, Carlos is not even here at Quarida de los Zorros. He hasn't been here for several months. And Bonnie is away, too — in *Norteamerica*."

"B-but you must believe me," Linn said desperately. "You can see I'm a captive here."

"Yes, that is what Margarita tells me," Carlota said. "I, too, was away, but she called and told me something strange was going on in my house so I came home. No one else knows I am here. I wanted to find out what is going on before I reveal my presence to Adella."

The older lady gazed at Linn. "Something *is* going on here, I will agree. But of one thing I'm certain: Carlos had nothing to do with it, and I doubt that my daughter-in-law did either. This Adella and I have never met, but maybe it is time I did. She is Bonnie's secretary, I understand, and she has an apartment near Bonnie's suite."

"Maybe Adella is not Bonnie's secretary at all," Linn said boldly. "Maybe she is really Bonnie, wearing a blonde wig and blue contact lenses. She is certainly the right size."

Carlota looked at her incredulously, but before she could say anything, Margarita spoke. "Pardon me for interrupting, but Adella is *not Dona* Bonnie. I have seen them both together. She takes care of *Dona* Bonnie's letters and invitations and that sort of thing. She was here before *Dona* Bonnie went to *Norteamerica.* She accompanied *Dona* Bonnie about the city, so others would tell you the same thing. *Senora* Adella is not *Dona* Bonnie. There is also the birthmark the secretary has. The *Senora* Bonnie has no such defect!"

Carlota listened gravely to Margarita's explanation, and then she turned to Linn. "Margarita will take you back to your room before you are missed. *Buenos Noches.*"

"B-but," Linn protested, "whether you believe Carlos is implicated in this or not, you *know* I'm being held against my will, and so is my baby!"

Carlota held up a soft jeweled hand. "That is true, but I do not know why. For all I know, you may have been caught stealing, and Adella is having you held until Carlos or Bonnie returns."

Linn tried to protest but Carlota was adamant. "Go with Margarita, now!" She turned her head away, and Linn knew the interview was over.

With leaden steps and heart, she followed Margarita back to her prison. On the way back, she tried to appeal to Margarita to help free her and Bobby, but the maid would not speak another word. She delivered Linn back into her room and went away with a sad smile.

After the secret panel slid into place behind Margarita, Linn spent a long time trying to find a switch or whatever the *criada* had used to get the wall to open, but she found nothing. The light had been too dim for her to detect what Margarita did to open the panel.

Finally, Linn lay down upon the bed. God had never seemed so far away. Carlota did not believe her story. There was no way out of her prison. And there were only two precious days left to be with her son.

My only hope is Carlota, and I'm afraid, she thought. *If Carlos is truly at the bottom of our abduction, and the leader of the kidnapping ring, it is very possible that Carlota won't risk prison for her son to help us.*

Or, if she does choose to help us, unless she moves quickly, that help may come too late. If

Adella gets wind of any interference in her plans, she could spirit Bobby out of the country. Clay and I would probably never see him again!

Fear and panic threatened to overwhelm Linn. Tears of despair came, and she wept for a long while. At last, her tears spent, she got up and paced the floor. Had the Lord deserted her? Why was He allowing her to go through such pain?

She tried to quote Psalm 37, but tonight the words seemed to mean nothing to her. She lay back down, but her torment and anxiety were too great.

Restless, she began to walk about the room again. In her mind's eye she could see Adella's jeering smile. She remembered Carlos as he was five years ago, heartless and utterly selfish. And Bonnie! Linn could still hear her mocking laughter. They were formidable enemies. Bonnie would have her promised revenge at last. A cruel, terrible one.

Suddenly Linn stopped her pacing. Bonnie! Adella! How much they were alike. Even though Margarita swore they were not the same person, they reacted to Linn in exactly the same way. The gloating and laughter Adella showed when Linn expressed anguish or pain was just what Bonnie would feel. It was all so confusing!

Scenes from many years ago flashed into her mind. God had accepted her, Linn — the rebellious one — and made her His child. He had brought Clay, her cynical husband, to a place of surrender to Christ and made their marriage better than ever before. Bonnie had tried to hurt her in the past, but God had *always* brought her through victoriously.

God had never failed her through the good times or through the bad. Now, when she was in deep trouble again, she was blaming God and doubting His ability and desire to help her. A wave of shame suffused her body.

Real faith does not have to see *the answer,* she reminded herself. *If a person could see the answer, then there would be no need for faith.*

"Forgive me, Father, for my unbelief and for blaming you," she whispered. "Whatever happens to me or to Bobby, I know you are with us. You are here right now! Not because I can feel your presence but because your Word says you are here. You live in me."

Peace like warm oil flowed into her spirit and spread through every atom of her being. She went to sleep with praises ringing in her heart.

17

It seemed to Linn that she had barely fallen asleep when something jarred her suddenly awake. Every nerve tingled with apprehension. The lock on her door was being softly turned. She could hear the key in the lock! Startled and afraid, she rolled out of the bed on the opposite side from the door and watched in fearful silence as the door opened without a sound.

In the pale light filtering in from the gallery, she saw a dark figure draped in a long robe slip into the room. A scream quivered in Linn's throat, but she dug a balled fist against her lips to stifle it. She crouched down behind the bed, her heart throbbing with fear.

Feverishly, she tried to recall if there was anything she could use as a weapon. In the darkness, she could see nothing. Then she remembered. There was a large clay vase nearby filled with flowers. Linn reached for it, carefully pulled out the bouquet, and wrapped one hand about its neck. Her heart whispered a frantic prayer, "Dear Father, please help me!"

For a full, throbbing moment the robed figure seemed to stand uncertainly just inside the door. Then it moved toward the empty baby bed on the far side of the room. Linn could see it bending over the crib and hear the rustle of hands upon the bedding.

Linn held her breath as the form straightened and moved around the bed. Low mutterings came to Linn's ears as she saw the figure run its hands along the side railing. Listening intently, Linn thought she could hear the word "baby" once or twice. She felt the hair raise on the back of her neck.

She didn't know whether to turn the light on or not The light would reveal the intruder, but Linn would also be clearly visible.

The figure was now feeling along the wall near the crib, still muttering softly. It seemed to be searching for something. Linn clearly heard the word "baby."

Moving along the wall, the form walked with a curious stiffness. When it reached the corner, it stopped in front of the large, low window that opened like a French door onto the gallery. Its head was facing the glass and for another long, tense moment it stood still. Then it turned in Linn's direction, and Linn could see the face. It was Adella!

Linn stayed very still. It was Adella, but she was acting very strangely. She moved to the end of the window with little stiff steps, feeling along with her hands. Then, abruptly, she stopped and spoke clearly but in an odd, halting way.

"Where-is-he? What-have-they-done-with-him?" Something that sounded like a sob came clearly to Linn's tensely listening ears. The figure moved into the center of the room. Then it moved again to the baby bed and bent over the empty crib, muttering indistinctly.

Linn felt her skin crawl. What was wrong with her? And where was Francesca?

Suddenly Adella raised herself and cocked her head as if she heard something. "Maybe she took him away," she said in the odd, childlike voice. "He's mine! I must get him back!" The figure moved toward the door, again muttering incoherently.

Walking with mincing, stiff steps, Adella moved across the room and out the door, closing it behind her.

Linn sprang quickly to the door. It was unlocked. Her heart quickened. Maybe she could find Bobby and escape! She opened the door and peered out. To her right, she could see Adella, moving with little choppy steps along the hall. When she disappeared around the comer, Linn eased out into the hall.

Then she heard the heavy tread of Francesca's feet coming from the opposite direction. Hastily, Linn drew back into the room and softly closed the door. She raced to her bed, jumped in, and drew the sheet up to almost cover her face. She heard Francesca try the door, then open it. Forcing herself to lie still, she heard the quick, heavy tread cross the room.

Francesca yanked the sheet away from Linn's face and shoulders. Linn could feel her black eyes intent upon her. Slowly, she opened her eyes. "What do you want?" she asked Francesca.

The big woman grunted, dropped the sheet top, and lumbered back out the door. Linn heard it lock behind her.

It was several minutes before Linn's heart stopped its mad pumping and her trembling ceased. Was Adella sleepwalking or was she trying to frighten Linn? It was a long time before Linn slept again.

In the morning, Adella strolled into Linn's room while she was feeding Bobby. "I just want to remind you that you have only one more day, after today, to take care of your baby," she said with a smile.

Linn laid the baby spoon down and turned her green eyes on Adella. "Were you in my room last night?" she asked peremptorily.

For a brief instant, a strange emotion flashed into Adella's deep blue eyes. *Was it fear,* Linn wondered. *Or shock?*

Then Adella laughed her husky soft tinkle and said nonchalantly, "Of course not, why do you ask?"

Though her tone was casual, her eyes, locked intently on Linn's, were not.

"Someone came to my room last night — dressed in a dark robe."

Was Adella's husky laugh a little forced? "And what did this ghostly person do?"

"Nothing," Linn replied. "Just walked around a bit, and then left."

"Your ghost didn't say anything?" Adella asked with a chuckle, as if she didn't believe a word of what Linn was saying.

"Just muttered something about a baby," Linn said. "And it wasn't a ghost. It was you! I got a good look at your face."

Adella walked to the door. Then she turned and laughed evilly. Twin devils danced in her velvet-blue eyes. "A little prank! I nearly scared you to death, didn't I? You are so amusing.

"Remember, there are only two days left. Then you can go home to your darling husband. I wonder if he'll blame you for not bringing back his son." A little ripple of husky laughter trailed behind her as Adella went out the door.

This time Linn scarcely heard it. She rescued the spoon from the floor where Bobby had thrown it, wiped it off on a napkin, and began to feed cereal into his mouth. Her thoughts were not fully on the baby. Had Adella only pretended to be sleepwalking or was the sleepwalking real?

Linn went over Adella's visit of the night before in her mind. It was still vividly alive. She could have been faking it, but somehow, Linn did not believe she was. And if she had been sleepwalking, it could happen again. Could a sleepwalker be dangerous? A shiver ran down Linn's spine.

18

Penny went to her room in a sulk after another argument with Kate. *Why can't mother let me run my own life,* she fumed. *If I make a mess of it, it's my choice.* She lay down across her bed. *If only I could talk to Bart!* His curly-headed good looks sprang quickly into her mind.

Suddenly she sat up in the middle of her bed, tucked her feet under her trim body, and exclaimed aloud, "I'll call him! He took my collect call the other day!"

A tingle of guilt touched her jubilance. Her call to Bart a few days ago had resulted in Bobby's kidnapping. But she shook it off. *If the kidnappers had been looking for an opportunity, they would have found one anyway,* she rationalized.

Springing off the bed, she went to the door and peered out into the hall. There was no one in sight. Swiftly, she ran down the hall to the *sala*. Picking up the receiver, she dialed the operator with cold, hasty fingers.

Within moments Penny heard Bart's mother on the line. When the operator asked if she would take Penny's call, the woman hesitated. Penny, suddenly frantic that she would refuse, said breathlessly, "I'll repay you for the call, Mrs. Youngblood — as soon as we get home. I *must* talk to Bart."

The operator interposed impatiently, "Will you accept the call, Mrs. Youngblood?"

Again Mrs. Youngblood hesitated, then said doubtfully, "I'll see if Bart can come to the phone." Again there was that tiny pause. "He has been a little under the weather."

"You *are* accepting the call, then?" the operator said with asperity.

"Y-yes," Bart's mother said. "I'll be right back."

Penny waited for several minutes as her stomach began to tie itself into knots. Would Bart never come? She didn't have a lot of money in her savings, and she couldn't ask Kate — or Jake — for money to repay Mrs. Youngblood for a call to Bart. A call she wasn't even supposed to make! This was twice she had broken her promise not to call him!

"Come on, Bart," she said aloud in exasperation, drumming her fingers on the black wood surface of the telephone table.

Suddenly Bart spoke into her ear. His voice sounded fuzzy and far away. "Hullo, Penny."

"Are you sick?" Penny asked anxiously.

"I'm all right," Bart said. The stilted monotone still didn't sound much like Bart's happy-go-lucky voice.

"Bart, I just had to talk to you. Bobby and Linn have been kidnapped and . . ." Penny's voice broke on a near-sob. "Bart, I'm just frantic. The police and Jake and Alfred and everyone are looking for them. But it's been five days, and there's no sign of them!"

Bart spoke again in that odd voice. "So old Jake is down there, too? Do you know what that old dude did? He fired me — from a job I didn't want anyway!"

A strange empty feeling yawned in Penny's stomach. "Bart, you told me you didn't take the job at Jake's ranch."

Bart hesitated so long that Penny said anxiously, "Are you still on the phone, Bart?"

"Yeah, I'm still here. But you caught me at a bad time. I was asleep."

"So you did work for Jake for a few days, like mother said?" Penny persisted.

"Sure-sure, for a few days."

"Bart, you lied to me. You said you didn't take the job. Why did you lie about it?"

"What difference does it make?" Bart said irritably.

"It makes a lot of difference!" Penny said hotly.

Penny heard a clatter on the other end of the phone as if Bart had dropped the telephone. "Bart? Bart, are you still there?"

"Silly old phone," she heard Bart mutter, then he said, "Can't seem to hang onto this wriggly old phone." He laughed, a loud burst of sound that dribbled into a giggle.

A suspicion burst into Penny's mind, and she voiced it in a shocked voice. "Bart, are you stoned on something?"

There was a brief hesitation and then Bart said defiantly, "What of it! If I want to take a little snort of cocaine now and then, it's none of your business!"

"Bart!" Penny said, stricken with horror. "You promised never to touch drugs again!" The cold, empty feeling in her stomach was making her feel slightly sick.

Bart's reply was blurred and sneering. "You sound just like that new dad of yours." His voice was high and unnatural. "He gave me a lecture on the dangers of drugs. The old goat! What does he know about real living?"

"Maybe more than you do!" Penny replied angrily. In her fury, she didn't realize she had defended her stepfather. "Bart, I won't marry a man who uses drugs! I told you that before!"

"Forget it then!" Bart said viciously.

The receiver slammed down with such a crack that it hurt Penny's ear. Dazedly, she replaced the receiver. Slumping down into a big chair, she stared at the telephone. Just like that Bart had terminated their engagement! Bart and she were through!

A pang shot through her. Bart had been lying to her all along! About using drugs and about quitting his job. The truth was a bitter taste in her mouth.

Suddenly she realized that tears were running in rivers down her cheeks. Tears for good-looking, good-natured Bart on a downward collision course with death or, worse still, with the living death of a drug addict. Tears for the shattering of her beautiful dreams of being Bart's wife. Tears for the once-so-close relationship with her mother that had deteriorated into an almost daily battleground. And tears of fury — at Jake for coming between them.

Penny curled into the comforting arms of the large chair and let her grief out in shuddering sobs. She felt humiliated and bruised by Bart's callous treatment. He had not even been concerned that Bobby and Linn were in the hands of ruthless kidnappers.

I doubt if it even registered in his drug-clouded mind, she thought bitterly. How could she have ever imagined he cared for her? Racking sobs shook her slender body.

Suddenly Alfred's voice called her name softly, and she felt his strong hand on her arm. His voice was anxious. "Penny, are you all right?"

Penny thrust her face more deeply in the chair unable to stop her tears.

"I've got a big shoulder, Penny," Alfred said softly, "and it's all yours, if you need it I've also got big ears for listening. Do you want to talk about it?"

"B-but I look a s-sight with my f-face all t-teary," Penny raised her head but kept it turned away from Alfred.

Alfred knelt and with a gentle hand turned her head toward him, awkwardly wiping away the tears. "You have never been anything but beautiful to me — even when you were thirteen," he said huskily.

Penny's head jerked up. Her tear-washed eyes looked into Alfred's with amazement. Five years ago, Alfred had followed her about with adoration. That look was mirrored again now in the warm brown eyes of

163

the twenty-year-old, attractive young man Alfred had grown into.

Penny dropped her eyes in bewilderment and confusion. Suddenly she felt warm and cared-for. "I-I was talking to Bart just now. We broke up."

Penny looked at Alfred covertly through wet, gold eyelashes. His eyes upon her were warm with sympathy, but he said nothing.

"My folks were right," Penny said miserably. "Bart has been lying to me all along about using drugs. He was higher than the Empire State Building just now — on cocaine."

"Does he mean a lot to you?" Alfred asked. "Do you really love him?"

"Yes, of course!" Penny said defensively. Then she looked away. Did she really love Bart? Or was he a part of her rebellion against Kate and Jake? She closed her eyes, and a vision of Bart rose into her mind's eye. He was moody — probably the result of his drug use, she admitted to herself now. But most of the time he was great fun to be with, joking and teasing and sweet. She had liked him a lot. Liked! The word shot through her. *Why didn't I say "loved"?*

Am I sorry that Bart is gone from my life? she mused. Yes, there was a void. Painful and deep in the freshness of the hurt. But of one thing she was sure: Even if Bart called and tried to make up when the drugs wore off, she knew she would never agree to it. She had more sense than to marry a drug addict or even an occasional user.

Her pride was deeply wounded, that she acknowledged even now. Bart had never spoken to her in the hateful, sarcastic way he had today.

Suddenly Penny felt extreme relief that she had called. If she had not called at just the wrong time, she might never have known — until after she married him — what Bart was really like.

Startled by the relief in her heart, Penny felt as if a great weight had been lifted from her shoulders. There was a faint feeling of sorrow for the passing of a fun playmate, but that was all.

She saw Bart clearly now, as if scales had been stripped from her eyes. Bart *was* a selfish freeloader who was pampered and protected by an indulgent mother — to his own destruction.

He had never kept a job because he didn't really want to buckle down and make his own living. Bart's father realized this. He had tried to rectify it. But Bart's mother, seeing him through the rosy glasses that Penny had also been using, stood firmly between him and his father's discipline and correction.

Penny looked at Alfred's clean-cut face so near her own, and suddenly she smiled. Alfred was not as cute as Bart, but he was already a man. A real man! Bart was a spoiled baby, and it was doubtful he would ever grow up. And just a short while ago, she would have married him in a minute!

"I thought I loved Bart," Penny told Alfred thoughtfully. "But now that I really think about it, I'm sure I do not. I would never even have dated a boy with his reputation if I had not been angry at mother. It's strange, and I can hardly believe it myself, but my main feeling about Bart now is relief that he's out of my life."

"My main feeling is relief, too," Alfred said with a grin. His lips were smiling, but his voice was firm as he continued. "I'm not rushing you, but I do want you to know how I feel. I was serious when I said I always thought you were beautiful.

"I still feel the way I did when I was fifteen and trailed you about with stardust in my eyes. I have dated a few girls, but none of them ever seemed to compare favorably with you. I care about you deeply, Penny. I always have."

Penny's eyes studied Alfred's lean face.

"You are sweet, Alfred," she said softly, "but my emotions are not easy to sort out right now. Could we just be good friends for now?"

"I'll always be that," Alfred said.

"Yes, I believe that! Thank you so much for being here when I needed you," Penny said earnestly. She laughed self-consciously. "I felt that my world had ended a short while ago, and now I feel like I've been reprieved from an awful fate. Thanks for caring, friend. I needed you to be here just now."

Grabbing her hand, Alfred squeezed it gently, but said nothing.

19

Later that day, Clay arrived in Veracruz. He looked like he hadn't slept for days. His eyes were bloodshot, and his handsome face was haggard. He had flown in, leaving Eric to drive the motor home on in to Veracruz.

Penny admired and loved her big sister's husband, and it was difficult to meet his eyes when he spoke to her. She still felt strongly responsible for Bobby's abduction. She blurted out immediately that she was to blame.

Clay's only answer was his usual warm hug and, "They would have found a way, whatever you did." Penny was relieved that he was not angry with her, but she was still miserable with strong feelings of guilt.

"I need a quick shower. Then I want to go down to the police station and find out if there have been any developments," Clay said. His eyes swept the group that stood about him in the large hall. "But first, I think we should all join in prayer together, asking God to direct us — and the police — in what to do and that He will bring Linn and Bobby back to us. There is strength in united prayer. And I know I need it right now. Is it okay with you, Esteban?"

"Yes, of course," Esteban replied quickly.

"Good! Let's join hands."

Kate, Jake, Josie, Alfred, and Penny moved forward to link hands. Esteban looked very uncomfortable but moved forward when he saw Alicia quickly move to stand in the circle.

"I will lead in prayer," Clay said earnestly, "and then if anyone else wishes to pray aloud, feel free to do so."

The few moments of concerted prayer by Clay, followed by Jake and then Josie, seemed to affect Esteban strongly. "Clay, my friend," he said, "I have never known people who talked to God as if he were a dear father — and friend. You act as if you really expect answers to your prayers. I truly hope you are right. But although I am deeply touched, I am also a little frightened. Perhaps when this situation is resolved, we can talk more fully about it?"

Clay gripped his hand fervently. "Esteban, I would like that — very much."

A few minutes later Jake, Clay, Josie, and Alfred left for the police station, and a thoughtful Esteban went to his office.

Penny, feeling somewhat left out of things, wandered through a hall she hadn't noticed before and found herself in a back courtyard. She knew the kitchen must be near because the pungent odor of fire-roasting chiles assailed her nostrils. She saw Luisa pinning clothes to the clotheslines strung in the courtyard. A basket heaped with wet clothes rested on the hard-packed ground.

Penny strolled over. "Hello, Luisa."

Luisa looked up and smiled her shy smile. "Hallo, Senorita Peeny."

There were six long lengths of clothesline. Penny began to pin clothes to the next line. For a few minutes they worked in silence. Penny was glad to have her hands occupied, and Luisa was obviously pleased with the help.

Penny finally broke the silence. "Luisa, what are we going to do? Nobody seems to know where to look for Linn or the babies. What if we never see them again?" Penny's voice broke. "I don't think I could bear that!"

Luisa stopped with a towel held in midair. Her plain face mirrored distress. "Please, *senorita,* don't cry. I'm sure they'll come back."

Penny sprang breathlessly to Luisa's side. "Luisa, what makes you think so?" Jake's assertion that he felt Luisa knew something she wasn't telling sprang into her mind.

Luisa's dark velvety eyes slid away from Penny's face, but not before Penny saw the wary look that crept into their shy depths. Luisa shrugged her shoulders and returned quickly to her work, working swiftly now instead of leisurely as before.

Penny returned to her place on the next line. She again began to lift the damp clothes from the basket and pin them to the line, but her thoughts were racing. *Luisa seems extremely anxious to get the clothes hung and away from me,* she mused. *And the way she answered so definitely that Linn and the babies would return. Was Jake right? Does Luisa know something about the kidnapping that she isn't telling?*

Penny dropped a pillowcase, with a beautifully hand-crocheted Mexican dancer border, back into the basket. Moving down the line of wet clothes to where Luisa was working rapidly, she laid her hand on Luisa's arm. "Luisa," she said gently, "you know who took Linn and the babies, don't you?"

Luisa refused to meet her eyes, and she

drew her arm away from Penny's touch. "No, *Senorita,* I don't know anything!" Her swift denial and averted gaze bespoke guilt to Penny.

Penny caught her by the arm again and shook it slightly. "Luisa, I don't know what you are afraid of, but if you don't tell us who took them or where they are, we might never see them again. They may kill them or sell them!"

"No! She won't, she . . ." Luisa stopped, terror written plainly on her face. "Please don't ask me about it," she implored. "I can't tell."

"Who are you afraid of, Luisa?" Penny asked. "The police will give you protection! I know they will."

"It isn't for me I fear," Luisa said desperately. "It is for Manuelito — my baby. If I say a word, the woman said she would cut out my baby's heart!"

"And she said your baby would be returned if you don't talk?"

"*Si — si!* So please, don't try to get me to tell you anything. The *Senor* Stone — he keeps trying to get me to tell him things but I cannot!" She ended in a pitiful wail.

Penny was thinking fast, excitement pulsing through her. "Luisa, how can you be sure this woman will do what she says? She

172

steals babies. The police believe she sells them for much money. People like that are not to be trusted. What would she have to gain by giving your baby back — except to lose the money he would bring her. I don't think she will give you back your baby, even if you don't say anything."

"No, no — she promised!" Luisa said, her face the picture of utter woe.

"But, Luisa, if you tell what you know, the police could get your baby back as well as Linn and her baby. Please, Luisa! I love my sister, and I'm terribly afraid of what they are doing to her and her baby."

"They will not be harmed!" Luisa said quickly. "The woman promised. . . ." Luisa clapped her hand over her mouth and moaned. Then she looked around fearfully and whispered, "They could be looking at me right now."

Penny put both of her hands on Luisa's shoulders and forced her to look at her. "What did the woman promise? Tell me!"

With a sob, Luisa sank down on the ground and put her face in her brown, work-worn hands. Penny dropped down on her knees in front of Luisa's trembling figure and said desperately, "Luisa, please tell me! The lives of Linn, both of our babies, and the other babies that have been stolen may depend on what you know."

Luisa only rocked in agony as she sobbed heartbrokenly.

Penny hadn't prayed in a long time. But she prayed now, silently and frantically. *Dear God, please show Luisa that she should tell me what she knows. If she doesn't, we may never see Linn, Bobby, or Manuelito again. Please, Father! I'm not asking for myself. I'm not worthy; but you are a loving God. Please, Lord have mercy on us — on me. I'm sorry for my disobedience that got us in this mess. Please, Lord. Please speak to Luisa.*

Aloud, Penny implored Luisa again. "Please, Luisa, tell me what you know."

Luisa, still crying softly and in deep anguish, shook her head in her cupped hands. Tears dripped off her hands and soaked into the dry, parched ground. From somewhere in the house Penny could hear the melodious caroling of Alicia's canaries. And nearby, the excited barking of a dog. Such common sounds seemed almost unreal to her when Linn's and Bobby's lives might be hanging by a thread. A thread that Luisa seemed to hold.

"Dear God, speak to Luisa right now and show her that she *must* tell what she knows!" Penny was unaware that she had prayed aloud until Luisa became very still and then raised her ravaged face to Penny's.

"You-you talked to God like you know Him," she said wonderingly.

"I do," Penny said earnestly. "I'm afraid I've been a disappointment to Him lately, but I still know He hears me when I pray." Suddenly, like a burst of dynamite exploding inside, she knew that what she said was true. *Forgive me, Lord,* she prayed silently, *for having such a hateful spirit these last few months.*

She felt the hard knot of rebellion in her heart begin to dissolve. Peace and relief seemed to flow slowly outward until even her toes and fingertips felt newly alive.

Penny did not know that her face radiated the joy that was surging inside her, but Luisa saw it. Penny saw only the change in the little *criada*'s countenance. "Because you know the *Christo,* I will tell you what I know, but you must promise not to tell anyone else."

"But Luisa . . ." Penny began to protest.

"You must promise," Luisa demanded stubbornly.

"I promise," Penny said quickly, fearing Luisa would change her mind.

Luisa took a deep breath. "*Senora* Adella Fernandez talked to me at the market a few days ago. She said that Manuelito would be returned to me if I would take a message to *Senora* Randolph."

"And you did?"

"*Si,* I took the message, and then led *Senora* Randolph out the back of the house and over a street or two into an alley where *Senora* Fernandez waited in a car. I left her there."

"Linn got into the car with Mrs. Fernandez?" Penny asked.

Luisa hesitated, and then laid her work-roughened hand on Penny's arm anxiously. "The woman told me that neither *Senora* Randolph or her baby would be hurt and that *Senora* Randolph and my Manuelito would be brought back here very soon at the same time."

"Did you wait to see what happened to Linn?" Penny asked.

"The *senora* told me to go away quickly after I brought *Senora* Randolph close to the car, but. . . ."

"You didn't leave?" Penny prompted.

"No. I slipped away and hid. When *Senora* Randolph saw that I was gone, she must have gotten frightened because she started to run back down the alley toward *Senor* Molinas's house. But the big black car came after her and a *mucho* big man grabbed her, put her in the car, and it drove away."

"Did you notice what kind of car it was? You know — a Ford, a Dodge, or what?"

"No, *Senorita,* only that it was *mucho* big and *mucho* black."

"Could you see if the Fernandez woman was really in the car?"

"Oh, *si!* ran along beside the car on the other side of an oleander hedge until it reached the street. They didn't turn on the lights, but when it came out under the street light, I saw there was a woman and small man in front. The woman was driving. *Senora* Randolph and the big man were in the back seat."

"You did really good!" Penny praised Luisa. "Can you think of anything else?"

Luisa grinned slyly. "In the detective movies, they always get the number on the car license."

"You didn't!" Penny exclaimed.

"*Si,*" Luisa beamed, delighted with her own brilliant foresight. Then she sobered. "I thought it might help to find her, if the *senora* did not bring back my baby." Slowly, she quoted the number to Penny.

Penny repeated the number several times. "I have it in my mind now." She hesitated. "Luisa, you must let me tell this to the police. They. . . ."

"No! You promised not to tell," Luisa cried.

"I know, but. . . ."

Suddenly a voice spoke from close by, and they both jumped. Jake moved out from behind a four-foot wall that bordered the garden, dusting loose dirt from his clothes. "I'm sorry to have listened, Luisa, but it may mean the difference between life and death for Linn and her baby."

Luisa jumped up. Her face had gone almost as ashy-white as one of the sheets fluttering gently in the breeze. "*Senorita* Peeny, you tricked me!"

"I didn't!" Penny denied emphatically. Her mind was in a turmoil, struggling with admiration for Jake's sleuthing success and irritation with him for spying on her and Luisa.

"No, Luisa," Jake said gently, "Penny didn't know I was listening. I had been wanting to talk to Penny so I decided not to go on down to the police station after all. I had Clay let me out of the taxi a few blocks from here. I walked back and started to go to Penny's room when I saw her head in the direction of the kitchen. When I saw her talking to you out here, I waited behind the wall. When I heard what you were talking about, I sat down to listen. And it must have been God's leading. Because Penny would not have broken her promise, yet now we have something to go on for the first time."

Luisa seemed to go to pieces before their eyes. She fell to the ground and began to weep hysterically, saying over and over, "You have killed my baby." Penny and Jake tried to reason with her, but her fear and anguish were too great.

"I'll get Mrs. Molinas," Jake said after a few minutes. Penny nodded as he hurried away. She kept trying to reassure Luisa but, fortunately, Mrs. Molinas came swiftly. She wrapped her plump arms about Luisa's shuddering body and led her inside the house. Meanwhile Jake put in a call to the police station and within minutes the police chief and several of his men arrived at the Molinas home.

This was the first break in the kidnapping cases and the police wasted no time in getting every fact possible from Penny, Jake, and also Luisa. At first, she refused adamantly to talk, but after a brief session alone with the dapper Chief Sanchez — what he said, no one knew — she told them everything. Her face was still ashen and stricken, but she seemed resigned.

Quite a while later, after she had told her part of the story, Penny slipped quietly out of the house and through the gate in the high wall. She felt she must get away from all the excited hubbub and sort out her feelings.

Penny walked slowly down the sidewalk toward a small public park where she and Linn had gone a couple of times, pushing Bobby in his stroller. Her throat constricted as she thought of Bobby and Linn. Thankfully, the future looked a little brighter now for them. Luisa's automobile license number and other information had been a real breakthrough.

"Dear God," she whispered, "please let us find them unharmed."

It was several blocks to the park and by the time she arrived, the stroll along the quiet cobbled street had calmed her nerves. Somewhere nearby she heard the haunting sound of a male Mexican voice lifted in throbbing, bittersweet song, accompanied by a guitar.

Entering the arched gate, she lifted her head and inhaled the heady perfume of a medley of fragrances. She could see many plants that she knew, planted in neat beds, artistically arranged. There were roses of every hue, poppies, gladiolas, orchids, and many other flowers. Flowering shrubs and large verdant trees gave shade along the flagstone paths. Honeysuckle and bougainvillea clambered over the stone wall that enclosed the park. Birds sang in happy abandonment, flitting about in the late afternoon sun.

For a few minutes Penny aimlessly followed a path that wound through the deserted park, reveling in the quiet beauty, and aromatic scents. Then she dropped to an ancient stone bench set beneath the shade of a towering tree, put her head on the back of the seat, and closed her eyes.

So many things had happened today! Her mind drifted over the events of the past few hours. A sharp pang knifed through her as she recalled the brief, agonizingly revealing phone call to Bart. But she refused to let herself dwell on that. Instead, somewhat to her surprise, a warm feeling swept over her as she recalled Alfred's earnest revelation of his feelings for her. When he was fifteen and she was thirteen, she had known he idolized her. But in the past five years, when she had seen him occasionally, he had been only casually friendly, nothing more. Hearing, abruptly, from his lips that this tall, intelligent young man had cared for her ever since, had been a surprise.

Tearing her thoughts from the pleasing image of Alfred's warm voice and steady dark eyes, Penny thought of Luisa. Pain filled Penny's heart for the torment that Luisa was going through. She honestly thought she had doomed her baby by confiding in Penny.

Father, please don't let that happen, she prayed silently. *Bring Luisa's baby back to her, and all of those other babies that this gang has kidnapped. These wicked people have brought terrible suffering upon the grieving parents of the infants that have been abducted.*

The sound of footsteps on the stone path near her aroused Penny from her reverie. She lifted her head from the bench back and opened her eyes. Standing before her were two young, shaggy-haired, Mexican men. Their black eyes were insolent and leering.

20

Penny stiffened, almost petrified with fear. She darted her eyes about and saw that she was absolutely alone with the pair. The men, one bean-pole thin and the other shorter and stockily built, were both dirty and unkempt. As if sensing her fear, they stepped closer so that Penny could have reached out her arm and touched them. The sour smell of alcohol reached her nostrils.

Drawing away, Penny said, with as much force as she could muster, "Please leave me alone." But her voice betrayed her and shook slightly. She knew now why Esteban had stressed that she and Linn were not to walk about Veracruz alone.

The shorter, heavier man leaned toward her and fingered a strand of her blonde hair with a dirt-encrusted finger. He said a few words in Spanish that caused the taller man to grin widely, showing tobacco-stained teeth with one missing.

Penny had never been more frightened in her life. Drawing on every ounce of her courage, she forced herself to remain calm. Silently, she implored God's help.

Suddenly she leaped to her feet, dodged the rough, reaching hands, and bounded away like a scared deer toward the entrance to the park. For a few yards, she heard their running steps behind her, and then she heard no more sound. She didn't dare pause to see where they were, she just ran with all her strength down the path.

She was just rounding the last bend in the path and could see the entrance arch. Relief surged through her. Putting on another burst of speed, she was within a few dozen yards of the entrance when suddenly the two Mexicans sprang out of the shrubbery just ahead of her. They must have taken a shortcut across the park! She darted out of their reach and jumped behind a stone bench.

The two men were breathing hard, even as she was. Like two predatory animals, their obsidian eyes glittered with the excitement of the chase as they began to move apart so they could hem her in. Penny felt a red haze of terror in her brain.

She heard a shrill scream, and it was a second before she realized the scream came from her own lips. She began to back away from the bench, her green eyes wide with fear. The two came on, silent now and intent on their deadly game.

"Stop!"

So engrossed were all three in the macabre drama that the harsh command brought the whole scene to an instant, poised halt.

Penny's head jerked toward the voice, and she saw Jake standing under a tree, breathing hard like he had been running. His hat was gone; his grizzled iron-grey hair was in disarray. His craggy face was set in stern lines, and his large hands were bunched into fists at his sides. "That's my daughter! You better not hurt her," Jake said sharply, his blue eyes bleak.

Without a word, Penny darted across the grass and cowered behind Jake's big frame.

With a savage, alcohol-enraged roar, the two Mexicans charged Jake as one man.

"Get back," he commanded Penny.

Penny backed away to stand partly sheltered behind the large trunk of a tree. Terrified, not only for herself but now also for Jake, Penny's breath came in frightened pants. *Those two animals will kill Jake,* she thought frantically. *Please, Father, help him — and me.*

Jake stood completely still until the savage thugs were almost upon him. Then one booted foot came up and struck the long, lean Mexican under the chin. He did a flailing flip through the air, landed on the grass, and lay still.

The stocky man leaped upon Jake and locked one muscular arm around his neck. Jake jerked his knee up into the man's stomach; with a gasp the man lost his hold, fell back, and rolled onto the grass groaning. Jake stood still, his blue eyes on both men alert and watchful; his large hands hung loosely at his sides.

Suddenly the stocky man rolled to his feet and crouched like a cougar ready to spring. A long-bladed knife gleamed in his left hand. Jake stood like a bulldog, his big head lowered slightly as he tensed for the attack.

A sudden shout reached Penny's ears, and she pulled her frightened eyes from the fight. A policeman was racing across the park, followed by two other men. The Mexican with the knife turned his shaggy head toward the sound. With a hoarse yell, he thrust his knife beneath his loose clothing and sprinted toward the entrance of the park. The policeman raced after him.

The other two men stopped near Jake, talking rapidly in Spanish. Penny leaned against the tree, her knees almost too weak to hold her up.

The two men, suddenly realizing that Jake could not understand them, shut off their flow of Spanish and conferred briefly with each other. Then one of the men, with a few words of English, some Spanish, and many gestures, informed Jake and Penny proudly that he and his brother had been sitting on a bench just outside the park when they heard the two men harassing the young lady. His brother had run down the street to get a policeman they had seen earlier while he stayed to keep an eye on things. He had seen Penny flee toward the gate and had followed until his brother and the policeman could arrive.

Just then, the policeman returned with a subdued and sullen captive. The officer introduced himself as Miguel Rios. By this time Penny had recovered enough to answer the policeman's questions of the attempted attack on her by the hoodlums. When she finished, Officer Rios asked Jake to tell his version.

"I saw my stepdaughter leave the house," Jake said, "and was concerned that she was going out alone. I followed her to the park but didn't let her see me since she apparently wanted to be alone.

"I sat down on a bench outside the far side of the park where I could catch glimpses of her following the path. Then I saw two men climb over the stone wall and drop down close to where I had last seen her. I started running across the park and then I saw her racing down the path with those two guys behind her. They cut through the park and caught her before she could get to the street. She jumped behind a bench, and they were stalking her like two wolves after a yearling," Jake said, his blue eyes blazing with anger.

The talkative Mexican spoke up. He had seen it all, he declared, and with many expressive hand gestures and rolling of his soft brown eyes, he eloquently told the story of the fight in a delightful mixture of Spanish and English.

After a while a police wagon came and took away the prisoners. When everyone had gone, Penny and Jake started back toward the Molinas's house. Walking with Jake, Penny felt flustered and uncomfortable. She had never really, in the four months Kate and Jake had been married, talked to Jake. What little she had said to him had usually been said in anger. Now this man whom she had always considered an interloper in her's and Kate's lives, had put his life in danger to rescue her.

She sneaked a glance at Jake's face and saw, to her amazement, that he looked as uncomfortable as she did. "Jake," she began hesitantly, "I-I don't know how to thank you. You-you probably saved my life. I have never been so scared before!"

She laughed self-consciously. "I never thought I would ever be glad to see *you!* But you looked like a knight in shining armor to me when you showed up."

Jake laughed. "I was a mighty scared knight about that time!"

"Honestly?" Penny asked in amazement. She had always considered Jake a braggart, with his booming voice and overpowering manner.

"Honestly," Jake admitted with a chuckle.

They walked on a few steps in silence. Suddenly Penny blurted out, "Bart and I have broken up for good."

Jake stopped dead still. He reached out, put his big hand on Penny's arm, and said gently, "I'm glad. That has been almost the death of your mother."

Sudden anger shot through Penny. "But why? She has you! She doesn't need me!" In instant regret, she could have bitten her tongue off. Why did she have to say such hateful things? Just today she had asked God to forgive her for such actions. Penny couldn't meet Jake's eyes which she felt intent upon her. She wanted to apologize, but the words seemed to stick in her throat. Pulling away, she started to move on.

But Jake took a firmer hold on her arm and wouldn't let her walk away. "That's it, isn't it? You feel that I've taken your mother away from you? I knew there was some reason you disliked me. That's what I've been wanting to talk to you about. Why you don't like me."

Penny felt her face grow red, and she refused to meet Jake's eyes. Glancing up through her eyelashes, she muttered, "It wasn't only that you took over my mother, but you kept trying to influence her against Bart. I knew he had used drugs, but I honestly thought he had quit. You-you even influenced mother and Linn to take me out here away from him. I-I just think you meddled in my affairs when it wasn't any of your business! I'm not *your* daughter!"

As though stung, Jake released her arm and began to walk down the sidewalk. Silently, Penny moved up to walk beside him. She looked covertly at Jake's face. It looked stern and angry. *I don't care,* Penny thought miserably. *He wanted me to tell him what I really think and then he gets mad!*

Suddenly, Jake stopped and looked at Penny. His voice was gentle. "Penny, let's sit down over there on that bus bench. There's something I want to tell you." He took her arm and guided her to the seat. Sitting down, he drew her down beside him.

Penny waited silently, her sober eyes on his strong, craggy face.

For a long moment he didn't speak or look at her. Then he sighed. "I haven't even told your mother this. It's very painful for me to talk about. I have a daughter!"

Penny started. She didn't know that Jake had been married.

"Her name is Jeannie," Jake said softly. He seemed almost to have forgotten her presence. "I was a pilot during World War II. My wife, Jerri, and I were married only three months when I was shipped out. I was flying missions over southern France when Jeannie was born. Two weeks later, Jerri had some complications connected with the birth and was dead at twenty-two."

"I'm sorry," Penny said softly, but if Jake heard her he didn't acknowledge it.

"When I came home, Jeannie was two years old. My mother was caring for Jeannie, and my dad had recently died, so I took over the ranch and we became a family of three."

Jake's voice dropped so low that Penny had trouble hearing him. "I had loved Jerri so much, and Jeannie was so much like her. She was what made my life bearable without my lovely Jerri. Jeannie became my life, and she felt the same way about me. We were very close and did everything together. She could ride like a boy and was my right hand man on the ranch."

A muscle twitched in his heavy jaw. "Then, when she was a senior in high school — seventeen years old, pretty as a picture, and as sharp as she was pretty — she met this guy."

Jake swallowed hard, and his voice turned bitter. "He was good-looking and several years older than she was. Jeannie fell crazy in love with him, even though she discovered soon enough that he not only used drugs but sold them as well."

Jake's big hands clenched and unclenched. "I pleaded with her, and reasoned with her, but there was nothing I could do. She married the guy and within six months was a drug addict." Jake's voice broke and Penny saw tears in his eyes.

Jake blew his nose on a big blue handkerchief and then looked into Penny's face.

"That's why I tried to do everything in my power to break you and Bart up. But then I remembered one of Jeannie's arguments: that I never gave her husband a chance. That's why I gave Bart a job. I know some addicts do quit — but unless they want help, there is no helping them."

"Where is Jeannie now?" Penny asked gently.

Jake suddenly looked ill, and he got to his feet like an old man. "She's been in a mental hospital for ten years," he said brokenly. "Her mind is irreversibly burned-up from all the drugs she abused it with. She's just a vegetable."

He looked away from Penny but not before she glimpsed the torment and pain deep within his eyes. "We'd best be gettin' back," he muttered, and he turned his steps toward the Molinas's house.

Penny stood for a moment and watched him go. Emotions churned and boiled in her. Suddenly, she ran lightly down the stone walk and caught up with Jake. Slipping her slim hand into his big calloused one, she said softly, "I can't take Jeannie's place, but I would like to be your daughter."

Jake stopped dead still and looked at her. His keen blue eyes misted, and he tried twice to speak before the words came out. "I'd like that," he said huskily. Reaching one arm around her, he hugged her close. "I'd like it very much!"

21

On the sixth night of her incarceration, Linn could not sleep. When the little nurse had come for Bobby at eight o'clock, Linn felt she could not let her warm, precious little son be taken away again. She knew the nurse cared for him well, and Bobby obviously liked her. But with only one more day promised to her, it seemed unbearable to Linn to be parted from her baby for the night.

She relinquished him only when the formidable Francesca stalked over and threatened by motions to take him by force. When he was gone, Linn paced her prison like a caged animal. Despondent, lonely, and troubled, Linn finally changed and climbed into bed.

But her mind would not turn off the questions and let her rest. Would Adella really take Bobby right out of her arms and sell him out of the country? Seeing Adella's face in her mind's eye, she knew she would. *I must get my mind off of that,* she decided, *and try to think of a way to keep it from happening.*

She knew Clay must have arrived by now. He, the police, and the Molinas household would be doing everything in their power to find them. *But will help come in time, if at all?* she thought. How she longed to see Clay and feel his arms about her!

Would Adella really release her after Bobby was gone? She must know that Linn would tell the whole story, wouldn't she? Strangely, Adella had not threatened her in any way if she exposed her and Carlos.

If only Carlota had believed her story! She was the only one who could help, it seemed, and she had refused to believe Linn.

I wonder if Adella will walk in her sleep again tonight? she thought. She shuddered. It was eerie to wake up and find the vindictive woman creeping about the room, muttering incoherently. It reminded her of Shakespeare's Lady MacBeth walking in her sleep! She shivered.

She had finally begun to slip into a light slumber when a faint sound brought her upright in the bed, her pulses racing. By the nightlight Linn had left on since Adella's sleepwalking episode, Linn saw the panel slide back and Margarita step out. Relief swept over Linn and excitement beat hopefully in her throat. Had Margarita or Carlota decided to help her?

Margarita wore a heavy shawl over her shoulders. She thrust another one into Linn's arms. "Take this and follow me quickly," she whispered. "*Dona* Carlota wishes to see you once more."

Linn quickly placed pillows in her bed again to resemble a person's form, threw on a housecoat, and slipped out behind Margarita. When they came out into Carlota's patio-garden, Margarita drew the shawl about her face and indicated that Linn was to do the same.

Linn prayed all the way to Carlota's suite.

She was shown into the mistress of Guarida de los Zorros's bedroom this time. The old lady was sitting regally in her luxurious bed, surrounded by big pillows. Linn thought she looked ill. Margarita drew up a chair for Linn and faded into the shadows somewhere behind her.

Carlota wasted no time in going right to her purpose for having Linn brought to her. "A reliable friend in the United States has been investigating your story. He said you are indeed Linn Randolph, with two children. One is visiting with your husband's mother in California, and the other, you and your sister brought with you to Veracruz to visit Esteban and Alicia Molinas.

"Inquiry in Veracruz has revealed that a Linn Randolph and her baby have vanished and are believed kidnapped. The police are searching for you both. Your husband, Clay, has arrived to aid in the search as well as your Aunt Kate Stone and her husband, Jake."

"Your investigation has been very thorough," Linn said, trying to speak calmly. Clay was so close and yet so far away! "So you believe now that my baby and I are being held here against my wishes?"

Yes, I do," Carlota said. "But I still do not believe my son has had anything to do with this."

"But Adella said. . . ."

"I know that Adella said Carlos was responsible for kidnapping you. But I still don't believe it. And until I find out the truth, I must not release you."

Linn felt despair flood her heart. Rising to her feet, she said as calmly as she could, "But you, too, will be a party to our kidnapping if you don't free us!"

Carlota raised her hand in a pacifying motion. "It won't be long until you are released, I assure you. But it is imperative that I wait for a certain event to occur before I free you."

"But Adella said she is taking away my baby tomorrow!"

"Did she, now?" Carlota pursed her fine, old lips in deep thought. "I will do what I can."

A tiny smile touched her lips. "I also checked out your allegation that Adella was really my daughter-in-law, Bonnie. But you are wrong. Apparently she knows nothing about your kidnapping either. She is in Denver, Colorado, following her favorite pastimes, traveling and shopping for new clothes." Disdain was evident in her tone. Apparently she wasn't enthralled with her daughter-in-law.

Linn's mind was in a whirl. "But-but if neither Bonnie nor Carlos are responsible for having us abducted, who is?"

"That I cannot say," Carlota replied. "Perhaps Adella planned this when she got herself hired as a secretary by my daughter-in-law. Maybe she knew that both Carlos and Bonnie were to be away for an extended trip and plotted to lay the blame on Carlos, if she got caught."

"But I recognized Carlos's two men!" Linn exclaimed. "They helped Adella kidnap me!"

Carlota shrugged delicate shoulders. "Maybe they are in this with Adella."

"There is more to this than Adella operating a baby kidnapping gang," Linn said stubbornly. "Adella seems to know me and has taken great pains to plot our abductions and the adoption of my baby so as to cause me as much pain as possible. And yet, I never met the woman before in my life! It doesn't make sense!"

Linn spoke urgently. "*Dona* Carlota, you must release me and my baby. Adella is a sadist! If she learns you are home, she may spirit my baby away; we might never see him again! Please! You must act now!"

Suddenly Carlota closed her eyes, and Margarita was instantly at her side. "*Dona* Carlota, I think this has tired you too much. I will take the *Senora* away."

The eyes fluttered open and Carlota motioned with a thin, veined hand. "Yes, I am suddenly very tired. Take her away." Her eyes closed again.

"*Dona* Carlota," Linn said desperately, "please help us!"

But Carlota did not open her eyes.

Margarita took Linn's arm and began to urge her quickly across the floor. But at the door, Carlota's faint voice stopped them. "I am sorry, *Senora* Randolph."

Margarita led Linn away. When they were again standing in Linn's room, Margarita said with a mischievous smile, "I see that Francesca has not been here."

Puzzled, Linn asked, "Were you expecting her to come in while we were gone?"

Margarita giggled. "Not really. She loves her wine and I added something to it to give her a good night's sleep." She chuckled. "I didn't want to risk getting caught by that Amazon. She's a mean one. I don't know why *Dona* Bonnie hired her in the first place."

"She's Bonnie's maid?" Linn asked.

"*Si,* Francesca went to work for *Dona* Bonnie shortly after she came here as *Senor* Zorro's wife. I don't like her, but she has always been *Dona* Bonnie's trusted maid. I'm surprised she would loan her to *Senora* Adella."

"That is odd," Linn agreed.

"I must get back to *Dona* Carlota," Margarita said. *"Buenos noches."* And she slipped away through the panel in the wall.

Linn sank into a soft cushioned chair near the bed, laid her head back, and pondered the things she had just learned. It was comforting to know that Clay was searching for her. He would not rest until he found her and Bobby. "Dear God, comfort Clay," she whispered. "He must be going through agonies. And give him wisdom. Help him to find us — in time."

She was still extremely puzzled about Adella. Why did the woman hate her so much? Had Bonnie somehow instilled that hate into her? Had Bonnie choreographed this whole diabolical plot from Denver? Was she going merrily about her shopping, laughing with glee for the suffering she and Clay were enduring?

But would Adella go that far for her employer? If she were caught, Adella would go to prison for kidnapping. And Adella acted as if this were her own personal vendetta against Linn and wanted Linn to know she and Carlos were behind it all!

It was strange. Adella had not tried to hide her identity from Linn. She had made certain that Linn knew she and Carlos and Carlos's two henchmen were deeply involved in not only her abduction but all the other baby-snatchings as well. It was very strange.

Perhaps she never planned to let Linn leave The Foxes' Lair. The thought tortured Linn, but it seemed a logical conclusion.

Carlota seems so positive that Carlos was not involved in this! Could she be right? Is Adella behind everything and setting it up to appear that Carlos is the real leader of the kidnapping gang?

Linn thought of the Carlos she remembered. Handsome and polite but with black eyes as cold as polar ice when he was angry. A chill crept down her back. She didn't agree with his mother! The Carlos she recalled would be capable of anything for money — or power.

Suddenly Linn heard a slight sound at her door. She sat very still, her heart hammering. It couldn't be Francesca, unless Margarita had misjudged the power of her sleeping potion.

A key turned in the lock as Linn tensed and sat waiting. A figure moved into the room and by the light of the nightlight Linn saw that it was Adella! And she seemed to be walking in her sleep again!

Adella was carrying a large object, wrapped in a baby blanket, in her arms. Moving with stiff, mincing steps, she walked to the baby bed and placed her bundle there. Humming a lullaby, Adele wandered about the room, touching the wall here and there as if searching for something.

Suddenly she stopped humming and said petulantly, "I'm looking for your bottle, so stop crying!" She hesitated, then began to feel her way about the room again, muttering incoherently.

But Linn was no longer watching Adella. Her whole attention was on the bundle in the baby bed. A sudden wild thought had taken possession of her mind. Was there a real baby in that bundle? Her heart thudded painfully. Maybe Bobby? Adella could hurt a baby in her sleepwalking state!

She rose from her chair silently. She had to see what was in that bundle! Could she reach the crib before Adella's ramblings took her back to its side?

So far Adella had not come near Linn's bed or the chair where Linn had been sitting. Linn eased her feet out of her shoes, crawled soundlessly across her bed, and put her feet on the floor on the opposite side. The bed gave a protesting squeak and Linn held her breath. Adella was still mumbling and bumbling along the wall on the far side of the room, near the gallery window.

Linn started tiptoeing across the room toward the baby bed, but Adella's words froze her. "You can't have him! Do you hear me, Linn? He belongs to Clay and me!"

Linn stood very still. How very odd for Adella to link her name with Clay's! Was she, like Bonnie, an old girlfriend from Clay's past?

Suddenly Linn realized that Adella was looking right at her. Her face was in the shadows, and Linn couldn't see it clearly. Could Adella see her?

Linn moved swiftly and silently. She reached the side of the crib and in one fluid movement snatched the bundle from the bed. Linn's heart almost leaped from her body. The bundle felt quite heavy, was soft, and moved when she lifted it out of the bed!

Linn darted back to her bed. She turned to see where Adella was, half expecting to see Adella's mocking smile. But the woman had resumed her muttering search about the room. Linn walked softly around her bed and held the bundle under the light of the nightlamp. With trembling fingers she unwound the tightly wrapped blanket. A plump Mexican baby lay in her arms, blinking up at her with startled black eyes!

Disappointment slammed her under the ribs. She had been so sure it was Bobby! She was aware now that Adella was back at the side of the crib as a moan of abject sorrow burst from her. "My baby," she sobbed. "She took my baby! I must find it." The woman moved out into the room, babbling unintelligently again.

Linn heard a bubble of sound and saw the baby's mouth pucker up to cry. Crooning softly, she put it against her shoulder. With a soft cooing sound, the baby snuggled into the curve of her neck.

I wonder if this is Luisa's baby? Linn thought. *What shall I do with him? I certainly can't let the sleepwalking Adella have him. She might hurt him.*

Suddenly, Linn heard a soft footfall near her door and held her breath as the door was pushed silently ajar. She expected Francesca's dark, frowning visage, but, instead, it was the face of Bobby's nurse that appeared. Her dark eyes were distressed, her brow furrowed with worry.

The dark eyes took in the room with one sweeping glance. She spoke rapidly in Spanish when she saw Adella. But when Adella continued to mutter, running her hands over the sides of the crib in a restless manner, the little *criada* put a small hand over her mouth in a gesture of dismay — and superstitious fear.

Linn was standing on the other side of the bed, holding the now sleeping child to her shoulder. When the maid caught sight of her, she exclaimed excitedly in Spanish. Keeping a frightened eye on Adella, the maid went swiftly to Linn, took the child from her arms, and left the room almost on the run.

Linn stared after her for a moment, and

then it dawned on her — *she left my door open!* Linn moved swiftly around the bed and across the room to the door. Looking up and down the hall, she saw that no one was in sight except the rapidly moving figure of the little nurse. Linn slid out into the hall and sped down the corridor after her.

The maid turned a corner. Linn raced silently behind her in her bare feet. Rounding the corner, she saw the nurse enter a room two doors down, to Linn's left.

Linn sprinted down the hall as softly as possible. She placed her hand on the door-knob and tried to turn it. The door was locked. She knocked softly at the door several times before a soft voice asked in Spanish who it was.

Summoning what Spanish she could recall, Linn answered as well as she could that she was *Dona* Linn and for her to open the door.

There was a short pause, and then the voice said in accented English, "*Dona* Adella say no one come in but her. I am sorry."

And no amount of coaxing could make her open the door. After a few minutes, admitting defeat, Linn turned back toward her cell with a heavy heart. Even if she could escape The Foxes' Lair, she would not leave without Bobby.

22

Passing Francesca's cot, Linn saw that she was still sleeping deeply, snoring loudly. The door of Linn's room was ajar and just before she reached it, Adella came out. She moved with an agitated gait, and Linn heard her mutter something about "my baby."

Adella turned and shuffled down the hall toward her own quarters. On an impulse, Linn decided to follow her. Darting back to Francesca's cot, she picked up the large flashlight that rested beside the bed.

Adella's robed figure was now almost to the corner and Linn hurried after her. Adella's suite was the first one beyond the corner. Linn was surprised to see her pass its door and go on to Bonnie's rooms. Opening the door, Adella passed through.

Linn ran lightly to the open door and looked in. Adella was moving on through Bonnie's luxurious sitting room into her bedroom. Scanning the room with cautious eyes to be sure no one else was there, Linn eased in and followed Adella on silent feet.

Standing at the door into Bonnie's sumptuous sleeping room, Linn was astonished to see Adella crawl into Bonnie's bed and stretch out with a sigh. Linn stood looking at her. In her sleepwalking, did she imagine she was the mistress of the household?

Then a realization hit her. The bed was already rumpled when Adella got into it. Adella was certainly making herself at home! She must be sleeping in her employer's satin-sheeted bed beneath a frilly canopy of exquisite beauty.

Adella seemed to be sleeping deeply now. A daring thought came to Linn. Carlos's room must be just beyond this one. Perhaps she could do some sleuthing while Francesca was out of the way and Adella was asleep. Maybe she could find some records in Carlos's quarters that would tell if he was involved in the kidnappings!

She quickly surveyed her surroundings. The door to her right opened into the study, she knew. The door into the large, lavishly furnished bathroom was open, so the remaining door probably connected this suite with Bonnie's husband's. Tiptoeing across the large room, Linn slowly turned the brass knob on the door. It opened easily and silently.

Glancing back at Adella, Linn could see clearly, by the light streaming in from the brilliantly illuminated gallery, that she was still sleeping. The large red blemish on Adella's face showed clearly. Linn felt a quick burst of sympathy. Aside from the blemish, Adella was very attractive. What a trial that birthmark must have been for her!

Passing into the other room, Linn pulled the door gently to and felt for a light switch. The gallery lights did not reach here. Her fingers finally felt the switch, and she flicked it on, revealing a short hall. Hurrying to the door at the end, she gingerly turned the knob. The door swung open without a sound.

Stepping into a large bedroom, she instantly knew that this was Carlos's room. It was definitely a man's quarters. Neat and orderly, the walls were done in cream, setting off the rich, deep red carpet that sank under her step. A king-sized bed dominated the room. Linn glimpsed red leather chairs, glowing mesquite furniture, and a huge fireplace with several guns hung over it.

She walked to the center of the room and gazed about. Where would a man keep records? Here in his bedroom or in the large sitting room she could see beyond? Her eyes found a desk near the wide window that looked out into the gallery. The drapes were partly open, letting in the gallery light.

Moving swiftly, she closed the drapes and turned on the flashlight. Carlos must be an orderly man, she thought. The top of the desk was absolutely empty. She began to pull out drawers filled with files, neatly arranged. She drew one out to examine it. It was the file of a tenant farmer.

She rifled through the other drawers. All contained records that pertained to the vast Zorro plantation. In the center of the desk was a drawer, and Linn pulled it out. Inside was a large book labeled "ledger." Linn opened it and caught her breath. The first page contained a list of names, Baby Garcia, Baby Urquiza, Baby Chavez, etc., each followed by a sum of money — large sums of money.

She turned to the next page and felt her heart flip. Names and addresses were recorded here with a notation of which baby had been sold to which person.

Linn's breath was coming in quick pants of excitement. *If only I could take down some of this information,* she thought. Then she remembered the paper and pens in the first drawer on her left. She slid the drawer open and then froze. She had distinctly heard a sound from the hall!

Pushing the file drawer closed, Linn stuffed the ledger into the middle drawer as quick as her now trembling fingers could manage. With quaking heart, she heard the sound of the door into the main hall being unlocked. There was no time to escape from the room!

She took two quick steps and slipped behind the drapes where the wall connected to the large gallery window. There was barely room for her slim figure in the corner where she stood. She was acutely aware of the fact that if she moved even a little, she would be outlined against the brightness of the gallery light outside the picture window.

Linn heard the faint, well-oiled swish of the door as it swung open. For a long moment there was complete silence, as if the person was surveying the room. Then, stealthy steps moved toward her across the carpet. Linn held her breath, fear beating in her throat. Had the person seen her slide into her hiding place?

The steps halted. Linn dared not move but her ears were keenly alert. She heard the drawers being pulled out and a slight sound as if fingers were moving through the files.

Then she heard a new sound — a slight scuffing sound.

Had the unknown person found the ledger? Linn carefully raised her right hand and pulled the drape slightly to one side so she could see.

A tall figure draped from head to ankles in a long, hooded robe was bent over the ledger lying on the desk. A light shown on the page. A low, almost inaudible whistle came to Linn's ears as the figure ran a finger down a column. Linn could distinguish fine, dark hair on the portion of hand she could see. The figure was a man!

Suddenly, a voice was heard in the small hall that separated the two suites. The dark-shrouded figure shoved the ledger back into the drawer, raced across the room, and out the door so swiftly that Linn could almost imagine there had been no one there. She heard the door close with a soft, muffled click.

Almost simultaneously, Linn heard the slap of feet moving rapidly through the small hall. A light flashed on and Linn heard a familiar voice saying irritably, "There is no one here, Francesca! You see?"

The heavy steps of Francesca and the lighter ones moved farther into the room. The familiar voice spoke again and Linn strove to recall whose it was. "Francesca, I ought to have your scalp for waking me up from a sound sleep! See? Nothing has been disturbed. You were imagining that someone was here."

Suddenly Linn's heart seemed to stop beating. Francesca's heavy tread was coming rapidly toward Linn's hiding place. What would they do to her?

23

Like a light snapping on, Linn knew that familiar voice beyond the drapes. It was Bonnie Leeds de Zorro! But Carlota had said Bonnie was in Denver — shopping!

However, there was no time to think about this discovery. Francesca, triumph gleaming in her black eyes, drew back the drapes that concealed Linn. The big woman spread her thick lips and uttered a hoarse burst of sound. Meant to express mirth, no doubt, it grated on Linn's taut nerves like fingernails scraping on a chalkboard. She grabbed Linn and hauled her out into the room as easily as if she were a rag doll.

But Linn scarcely noticed the roughness. Her green eyes widened in astonishment as she saw that the only person in the room was Adella.

Adella's husky, throaty voice said softly,

"So Francesca was right. Someone *was* in here prowling around."

Linn was staring at her. Her eyes darted about the room and came back to Adella. Incredulity shone in her face as she said slowly, "You *are* Bonnie! I should have known!"

Her mind was racing. But how could Adella be Bonnie? Margarita and Carlota had both said Adella had been here at the same time as Bonnie. And Carlota said she had proof Bonnie was in Denver. Yet the voice she heard a minute ago was Bonnie's!

For a long moment Adella's velvety-blue eyes locked with Linn's. Then she laughed. Not the tinkly laugh of Adella but Bonnie's laugh. "So you guessed? Well, it was about time for me to reveal myself anyway. I wouldn't want you to leave here without knowing who dreamed up this scheme of all schemes to make you suffer!"

Bonnie laughed softly. She was obviously enjoying herself.

Bonnie waved her hand toward her own quarters. "Come into my rooms. We might as well be comfortable while we have a little chat."

Francesca took Linn's arm and pushed her ahead through the small hall; Bonnie followed. Then Bonnie led the way through her bedroom into her sitting room.

"Sit down," Bonnie ordered Linn. "You may go, Francesca," she told her big *criada*.

Francesca hesitated. She plainly did not want to leave her mistress alone with Linn.

"Go!" Bonnie ordered. "You may wait in my office until I call you to take the *senora* back to her room."

Frowning, Francesca went out and closed the door.

Bonnie turned toward Linn, her blue eyes filled with laughter. "I can see you are dying to know how and why I set up this whole thing about being Adella. Well, I'll tell you about that, but first, I want to speak of something I know is closer to your heart. I understand you have two children now. Children of Clay's that should have been mine!" Bonnie's face distorted with unmasked malice.

In spite of herself, Linn felt fear trace its icy fingers down her back. There was an almost maniacal gleam in Bonnie's eyes. She reminded herself, as she had in the past, *Bonnie is an actress and a good one. She is in control of herself at all times. Standing back and watching her audience, she always tries to manipulate their emotions — and she usually succeeds.*

But this time Linn sensed a subtle change

in Bonnie. Had Bonnie played at being a little insane for so long that she had actually become mentally deranged?

Linn chose her words carefully. "Bonnie, you are married to a handsome, wealthy man who loves you. You should be very happy. Why do you still blame me for marrying Clay? I did not even know you or know that you had been engaged to Clay when I married Clay. And he asked me to marry him. I didn't take him away from you. He took himself."

Linn swept her hand out. "Look at all this beauty and luxury. A princess would envy you!"

For a moment Bonnie's eyes still smoldered with malice, then it vanished. Her eyes suddenly glowed with affection and warmth. "You are right, of course."

"Will you please give me my baby and let me go?" Linn asked softly.

Bonnie eyed Linn; a small twitch hovered at the corner of her mouth. "You would like that, wouldn't you? Just take him and go. Then you and Bobby, your little daughter and Clay would live happily ever after — just like in the fairy tales." Her face suddenly twisted with fury. "Well, this is not a fairy tale! This is for real! *I* have your son — Clay's heir and the one who bears his name.

And you can never have him back!"

Linn's heart twisted. "Bonnie, this is crazy! Hurting me and Clay will not bring you joy. Please give up this wild scheme and leave us alone. Please, Bonnie!"

Bonnie's laugh was high and shrill. She sounded a little mad. "No! I promised you seven days with your baby, and the time is up in a few hours. I have kept my promise."

"W-what are you going to do with Bobby?" Linn tried to keep her voice calm. She knew Bonnie was baiting her.

Bonnie's chuckle was soft now, her voice the husky voice of Adella. "Oh, I have this planned to perfection! Didn't you like my role as Adella Fernandez?"

Linn said nothing.

Leaning her blonde head back against the forest green velvet couch, Bonnie continued. "You see, this plan is bigger than just keeping that promise I made to you eight years ago. You do remember that promise?"

"What promise?"

Bonnie laughed, tinkly and lightly. "Don't play dumb! You remember. I promised to make you wish you had never been born if you kept me from marrying Clay!"

Linn tried to match Bonnie's lightness. "That was so long ago that it's ancient history. You are happily married and so am I.

It's time to forget the past and move on."

Different emotions seemed to flicker over Bonnie's face, like pages turning rapidly: bitterness, discontent, hopelessness, deep resentment, even self-pity, an emotion Linn would never have associated with the always-in-control Bonnie. "*You* are happily married. I married a devil!"

"But — what about — I'm sorry," Linn finally said, unable to piece together exactly what Bonnie was saying.

"Don't be!" Bonnie said spitefully. "*You* are the one who needs pity, not me. My plans for your life are not pleasant!"

Linn's heart lurched with fear. She knew only too well that Bonnie was a dangerous woman. She kept her eyes on Bonnie and said nothing, but in her mind a fervent prayer went up. *Father, help me to stay calm. Give me wisdom in how to conduct myself with Bonnie. And please, set us free of this woman!*

Bonnie stood up and leaned toward Linn; a malicious, mocking smile twitched her lips. "I promised to make you sorry you were ever born, and I think this is the perfect plan! An exquisite torture that will slowly destroy you over each second of each year that you live. You will suffer every day for the rest of your life!" She paused dramatically, then sank back down in a peach velvet lounge chair.

She's purposefully drawing this out to hurt me, Linn thought, *and it's doing just that!* Linn's stomach had knotted and every nerve was taut. She began to have trouble breathing; the room seemed to be closing in upon her. She felt like she was drowning. *Help, Lord!* The cry came from deep inside her.

Suddenly a thought rose to the surface of her mind. God had promised never to leave her or forsake her. He was here — right now! God was still in control. A tiny bubble of joy seemed to form inside her, calming her jagged nerves and smoothing out the knots in her stomach.

"You will never get away with this!" Linn said. "You know I will tell the police!"

"Tell them! But if you do, do it with the knowledge that you are sealing your baby's doom. I will kill him before anyone can rescue him!"

The color drained from Linn's face. "Even you would not kill an innocent baby."

"Try me! You know I will, if I have to!" Bonnie's voice dropped to a husky purr. "But I don't think I will have to kill that adorable baby. Mom and Dad Randolph will not report who took their child. It would be hard to prove anyway! Remember —

Bonnie is being seen daily in Denver, Colorado! And you are on my turf; you are in Mexico. My in-laws are very powerful and rich. You are *gringos* from *Norteamerica*."

Linn knew that what Bonnie said was true. It would be her word against the testimony of a rich, powerful Mexican family.

She was unaware of the tears running down her face until Bonnie laughed softly. "Cry, Linn, cry! Your eyes will become fountains of tears! Every day of your life you will grieve for your baby. You will wonder if I put him in a good home or in one where he will be abused. Will he have enough food? Is he being beaten?"

Linn stared at Bonnie with stricken eyes.

With a wicked tinkle of mirth, Bonnie continued. "I see my plan is more successful than my wildest dreams."

"You-you are evil!"

"Yes, I suppose I am," Bonnie said with satisfaction. "And have you thought about what will be the hardest part of this life I have plotted for you? You will never know — anything about him. You will wonder what he looks like as a little boy. How he develops in school — if he is sent to school. What he looks like as a teenager, a young man. Who and if he marries. His life will be forever severed from yours! It is the ultimate punishment, and I decree it for you, Linn Randolph!"

Again, Linn wondered if Bonnie was mad. Had her hatred driven her over the brink of insanity?

Linn had a sudden thought. "Surely Carlos — your husband — will not condone and allow you to carry out this scheme!"

Bonnie laughed, without mirth. "Carlos does not know! He is not home." Her voice became a brittle thread of bitterness. "He isn't ever home!" Her voice rose, and Linn again wondered if Bonnie was hovering on the brink of insanity. "He isn't aware that I know about that dark-eyed dancer he spends his time and money on! I have even seen them together!"

Bonnie seemed to have forgotten Linn. Her face twisted with passion, and her eyes glittered with malevolence. "But I have arranged a little surprise for him, too, when he arrives back at Guarida de los Zorros! And that philandering fox has it coming!"

Bonnie's voice sunk to a conspiratorial whisper. "I have framed him! Even *he* won't be able to squirm out of this! And Mama Fox will not be able to rescue him this time!"

Linn remained silent

Bonnie laughed slyly, in sadistic glee.

"*Don* Carlos has spent so much time with Violeta that he is not aware a kidnapping ring has been operating for three months from The Foxes' Lair. Black market babies sell for fifteen to twenty-five thousand dollars apiece to childless Mexican couples with more money than sense!

"Of course," Bonnie said cunningly, "since the black market traffic has all been connected with Carlos's ancestral home, I felt it only proper to deposit all the money in his personal savings account. And to make it easy for the police to know who has been stealing and selling those sweet innocent babies, Adella, his little helper, kept a good record. It's in Carlos's desk — as I'm sure you discovered."

Linn chose her words carefully. She didn't want to give away the fact that Carlota was looking into things. "But when the police come, they will catch you, too. Won't they?"

Bonnie chuckled, and her eyes danced with merriment. "I'm not here! Remember, I'm Adella. Let me tell you how I arranged all of this. It took a bit of searching, but I found a woman who looked a lot like me and was built like me. But she, also, does not look like Adella. She's brown-headed and has dark brown eyes. I got her a wig and blue contact lenses, and we concocted this beaut of a birthmark.

"Then I had her come to The Foxes' Lair looking for a job as secretary — in answer to my ad. I hired her while dear Carlos and Mama Carlota were here, made certain Carlos met her, and saw her around a month or so before he left again — supposedly on business, but really to be with Violeta again." Bonnie's eyes narrowed to blue slits of anger.

She hesitated and got up to pace about the room with agitated steps. Then she came back and stood before Linn. "You see, I have planned this well and thoroughly. I have been working on the plan for at least a year. Ever since I discovered why Carlos was spending so much time away from home!"

"I'm sorry that Carlos is unfaithful to you," Linn said.

Bonnie drew in her breath sharply and turned away for a moment. "Carlos is a beast!" she said savagely. "Selfish, hot tempered, jealous, and cruel. He even struck me once when we were arguing. But he had better never try that again!" Bonnie turned to face Linn. Her hand slid inside her robe and when she drew it out, a slender-bladed dagger lay shimmering in her palm. "I'll never take a beating from a man! Never!

"I considered divorce, but decided I wouldn't allow him to get away that easy. He could be with Violet all the time then. So I came up with this beautiful plan to pay off my debt to you — and my dear unfaithful husband at the same time!"

In spite of the situation, Linn marveled at Bonnie's shrewdness in planning. "You didn't finish telling me where Adella fits into this scheme," Linn said.

"Oh yes, Adella. She plays a very integral part. After she became an accepted member of the household, I wore blue contact lenses I had had made for myself and Adella's wig. We removed her birthmark and applied an identical one to my face, and I took Adella's place. She put on a replica of my dark hair, removed her contact lenses, and happily left for a few months of shopping in Denver and some other places."

Bonnie giggled. "I am registered at an expensive hotel and am seen daily about the city, buying clothes, dining, seeing the sights, making travel arrangements for weekends in Aspen, Dallas, and even Los Angeles."

"While *you* have been here at Guarida de los Zorros posing as Adella and Carlos's accomplice in a kidnapping ring," finished Linn.

"Clever, isn't it?"

"But won't Adella be left holding the bag?" Linn asked.

"There is no Adella," Bonnie said. "This woman has no criminal record, so her fingerprints are not on file. I — as Adella — will leave the house at the same time as you, remove her disguise and don a new one — which I don't plan to reveal to you — and vanish across the border into the United States.

"The lady who is impersonating me will remove her disguise, essentially vanishing, and I will step into her place, continuing my stay at the hotel in Denver for a few more days. My double will return to her life again but with much more money to see her through the hard places."

"And you plan for Carlos to be arrested as the kidnapper." Linn said. "I suppose the police will get an anonymous tip to steer them to The Foxes' Lair?"

"Precisely! They will be very grateful for the help in cracking the case."

Suddenly Bonnie dropped her light bantering tone and spoke crossly. "Enough of this! I'm tired. I'll call Francesca to take you back to your room."

"You walked in your sleep again tonight, Bonnie," Linn said softly. "Did you know that?"

A strange expression crossed Bonnie's face before she said, too quickly, "Just a little scare tactic!"

"I don't believe so," Linn replied thoughtfully. "I think your mind is troubled. Both times you came, you were muttering about babies. This last time you brought in a plump little Mexican baby. Was that Luisa's baby? Did you get her to bring me a message by promising to return her baby if she helped?"

"I don't care to continue this discussion," Bonnie said stiffly as she rose to her feet.

"What if someone pressures Luisa into telling what she knows?" Linn continued. "Your little ball of yarn could begin to unroll, and you would be caught in its strands. Bonnie, forget about all this revenge stuff and let Bobby and me go."

"Never!"

"Bonnie," Linn said earnestly, "hate is like a corrosive acid. It can harm others, but at the same time it corrodes at the one who harbors it. Let the Lord help you get rid of it before it wrecks your life and health."

A maniacal fire seemed to leap into Bonnie's eyes, and Linn saw her hands clench into hard white fists. Her voice was shrill as she lashed out, "Don't talk about God to me! You are so pious! You stole my husband and bore him the son that should be mine! You will pay!"

"He was never your husband," Linn said gently, "only your fiance."

Bonnie raised her hand and opened it as if to strike Linn. Then, abruptly, the hatred vanished from Bonnie's eyes and she lowered her arm. Now Bonnie's eyes were warm and her voice friendly.

"Linn, dear, it is time to go. Tomorrow will be the last day of your life — with your son. You need your rest so you can enjoy it. Adella will come for him at some point tomorrow, and she may even have a little ceremony to celebrate the occasion. Yes! That's what she will do! When it is prepared, Francesca will bring you to the celebration!"

With a tinkle of laughter, she turned from Linn and called, "Francesca! Come and take Linn to her room!"

Suddenly Linn was very tired As she went with Francesca, she felt as if each foot was weighted with lead. Had God forgotten where she was?

24

Francesca took Linn to her room and left immediately, locking the door behind her. Linn lay down on the bed without changing to her nightgown. She was so emotionally exhausted that she felt she could not hold her head up a moment longer.

But almost as soon as she lay down, her mind grew alert and wakeful. She must find a way to escape and take Bobby with her!

But she had tried the doors and windows repeatedly. Besides, she could not go without Bobby. Bonnie might do anything to him in revenge. Better to have him alive and with new parents than dead!

Maybe she could talk to Margarita in the morning when she brought their breakfast. Carlota had to be made aware that time was running out!

Suddenly, she remembered something. Who had been looking at the record book that Bonnie had placed in Carlos's desk with information on the adoptions of the kidnapped babies? Could that have been Margarita? No, Margarita was short and small. Besides, it had been a man's hand that she had seen.

Could Carlos have returned? He would hardly be sneaking about in his own quarters. And if Carlos had returned, he would be unlikely to help her. She had been instrumental in nearly having him sent to prison five years ago. She recalled his cold, handsome face and shivered. *I hope that intruder wasn't him,* she thought.

Her mind shifted to Bonnie and her plot. Her heart quavered with dread. The plan was brilliant, she conceded. If it succeeded, Bonnie could strike back at Carlos for his infidelity and at Linn for her imagined wrongdoing. Bonnie's vengeance would ruin both of their lives.

Please, Lord, she cried in her heart, *stop Bonnie before she hurts anyone else.* Linn fought to leave it in God's hands, but it seemed that she could find no peace. Tomorrow would be the worst day of her life, if God did not intervene.

She thought of her son. Bobby loved everyone and never saw a stranger. Her heart swelled with pain so great she could scarcely contain it. She could not lose Bobby. She couldn't bear it!

Then a thought edged into her mind. Was this how the heart of God ached and throbbed with anguish when He saw Jesus offered on the cross? Was that why the whole earth reeled as if in agony? Had God covered the scene with darkness so He would not have to look at His Son writhing in pain as the sins of the world rested on His lacerated back and He hung suspended from that cross of shame?

Suddenly Linn felt the burning of shame. Even if she never saw Bobby again, she knew he would not have to go through what Jesus, God's Son, endured. *And the Spirit of God will be with me through whatever I have to endure!*

An enormous peace swept over her agony and Linn slept.

She awoke to the sound of the door being unlocked. As the door swung open, Francesca entered with Bobby draped over her arm. Linn ran to take him from her. Francesca seemed relieved to surrender him. She dumped some baby clothes in a chair and departed, locking the door. Bobby chortled happily as Linn held him, planting a soft, wet kiss on her face.

Bobby's diaper was soaked for the first

time since they had been there. *Where is his nurse?* she wondered. She would ask Margarita when she came with breakfast. Not that Margarita would probably be allowed to answer her!

Linn was bathing Bobby, and he was splashing water all over the place when breakfast arrived a few minutes later. But Margarita did not bring it; Francesca did. The tray was sloppily arranged, and the food poorly prepared. Obviously, Margarita had not cooked or arranged it on the tray.

As Linn set the plate of runny eggs out on the table, she saw a note beneath the plate. Printed with pencil, the scrawled words were from Bonnie.

Linn,
No servants will mar your last day with your son — except Francesca. I haven't decided yet when I will come for your baby and release you to your son-less fate. Count the precious hours for I will *come! I'm looking forward to our little ceremony!*
Adella

Linn felt as if a knife had been plunged into her heart and twisted. Adella — Bonnie — was a sadistic monster!

The day dragged by in agonizing slowness. Francesca brought food three times and departed quickly each time. Linn's nerves stretched taut from listening for Bonnie's footsteps.

Eight o'clock passed, the time Bobby's nurse usually came for him, but no one appeared. Nine o'clock came and then ten. *Bonnie is dragging this out to make it as dreadful as possible,* Linn thought. She would almost welcome her footsteps now to relieve the pressure that was building — building in her mind and body.

Linn had put Bobby to bed at nine — tired and complacently happy, unaware of what his mother was going through. Linn sat in the small rocker, praying and quoting Scriptures to herself. She was glad for the psalms and other verses she had memorized.

I wonder if this is how a person on death row feels as he awaits the hour of death, she thought. *No! No! I must not be morbid!* Slowly she began to quote the 23rd Psalm aloud

She was not aware that she had fallen asleep until she heard Bonnie's voice in the room. Springing up, she saw that Bonnie — her Adella disguise intact — was dressed for travel. Her honey-blonde hair was plaited into a single braid down her back. Linn glanced at the clock. It was one o'clock.

"My — my!" Bonnie ejaculated. Her voice held disapproval. "Does losing your son mean so little that you could fall asleep while you waited?"

25

Bonnie said companionably, "Let's go to my quarters. Our little ceremony is all prepared." She turned to go and then turned back. "There is a bag packed for the baby; formula and everything he will need is already in the car. Bring him and come."

Linn picked sleeping Bobby up out of the crib carefully. He sighed, yawned luxuriously, and then snuggled against Linn's shoulder. A huge lump formed in Linn's throat, and she swallowed hard. Would she never see or hold her son after tonight? Almost angrily, she thrust the thought away. A clear mind was her best weapon right now. Surely there would yet be a way of escape.

"Come on!" Bonnie's voice betrayed irritation.

Carrying Bobby, Linn followed her out into the hallway. There was no sign of Francesca or any other servant. Her heart leaped with hope. *I'm larger and stronger than Bonnie. Unless she has help, Bonnie cannot take my baby from me!*

Entering Bonnie's sitting room, Linn stopped in horror. The room was lit only by candles — four long black ones. Black streamers hung from the unlit chandeliers. Most of the room was in deep shadows, giving it an eerie, unreal quality. The drapes were drawn tightly against even a speck of light — or air, it seemed to Linn.

Bonnie clutched Linn's arm and guided her to a small table where a rectangular object about three feet long rested, draped with a heavy black cloth. At each end of the table stood two unlit black candles.

"Stand here," Bonnie directed, placing Linn — still holding her sleeping baby — in front of the table. Removing a lighted candle from its holder, Bonnie came back and lit the two on the table, slowly and ceremoniously. Prickles of apprehension ran over Linn's skin.

"Now," Bonnie said, "we are about to begin the ceremony." She stepped between the two long black candles on the opposite side of the table from Linn and Bobby. "Remove the cover, Mrs. Clay Randolph." She motioned with a slim, jeweled hand to the black draped object.

Her heart pounding, Linn reached out her hand, keeping it steady with great effort. She lifted the edge of the drape gingerly.

"Pull it off!" Bonnie ordered.

Linn yanked it off. A gasp burst from her lips and the cover dropped unnoticed from her suddenly nerveless fingers. The object was a small white casket!

Linn felt her knees go weak and a humming noise seemed to fill her brain. If she didn't sit down quickly, she knew she would faint. She backed to a chair she had seen behind her and sat down heavily.

Bonnie's mocking laughter suddenly filled the room — high and shrill. "Don't you think the casket is a fitting touch to your farewell ceremony to your son?" Her laughter floated out again and raked like claws on Linn's taut nerves.

Then Linn felt Bobby wriggle in her grasp, and she realized she was holding him too tightly. He whimpered sleepily, and suddenly, it broke the spell that had enveloped Linn since she entered this room. An atmosphere Linn knew Bonnie had carefully planned to frighten her out of her senses.

Linn stiffened and drew in a long breath. She was a mother and responsible for the well-being of her child. God had given her the privilege of motherhood, and she would give it her best!

Strength seemed to flow back into Linn's body. She stood — on slightly wobbly legs but gaining steadiness by the second — and moved to the side of the table facing Bonnie. Her voice was calm when she spoke. "Cut out the dramatics, Bonnie. I'll not take part in this ridiculous ceremony, as you call it!"

Her green eyes glowed with a fire to match Bonnie's as she faced her across the table. Steadily she defied her adversary, without flinching or blinking. For a long poignant moment they stood there, eye to eye, with the little coffin between them.

Anger had flashed into Bonnie's eyes at Linn's words. The eerie, shadowy room seemed charged with surging currents as she stared into Linn's green eyes. After a moment, Bonnie laughed, almost companionable again. "Well, at least you have guts! Not that it will get you anywhere!"

She stared at Linn for a long moment, then said abruptly, "Open the coffin lid and place the baby in the coffin!"

Linn stared at her. A tremor ran through her, but she stood her ground. Her jaw tightened. "I will not!"

Fury sprang into Bonnie's eyes; her lovely face twisted as she screeched, "You will!"

"I won't!" Linn said calmly, hoping the trembling that was beginning again in her knees was not obvious.

"Francesca!" Bonnie shouted.

Instantly the big form of Bonnie's *criada* materialized from the shadows behind Bonnie.

"Take the baby from Linn and put him in the casket!" Bonnie ordered.

Francesca's eyes widened and fear shone in her dark, ugly face. She grunted unintelligibly and backed away.

Bonnie's face registered shock — and outrage — at her maid's disobedience. She spoke sharply. "Do as I say! Put the child in the coffin!"

Francesca rolled her eyes in fright as she took a step forward, then she retreated from the coffin again, her hands raised as if to ward off evil spirits.

"Your servant is afraid of the coffin," Linn said. She hesitated, and then she added softly, "Bonnie, you also need to fear the death it represents. Hate and vengeance have ruled your life. If you die in this condition, you are doomed throughout eternity. Your money and power will have no affect on God."

Linn's eyes shone emerald green in the soft candlelight as they locked with

Bonnie's. She stood as if mesmerized as Linn continued softly, "God requires so little of you and me. Just to confess that we have sinned and need God's forgiveness, and then to accept Jesus Christ as our Saviour. As you well remember, I'm sure, I almost wrecked my marriage with suspicion and hate. But God took away the hate and the desire for revenge. He wants to do the same for you, Bonnie."

Suddenly, Bonnie moved jerkily, almost as if she were shaking herself. Then she threw back her head and laughed shrilly. When she finally stopped, she said lightly, "Linn, if you don't beat all! If you were being led to the gallows, you would stop everything and try to convert the executioner!"

Suddenly her voice hardened. "But it wouldn't affect that executioner and neither will it affect me! I am going to take away your baby and with him will go your desire to live. Yours will be a living death!"

Fear again tore at Linn's insides, making her heart hammer and convulsing her stomach until she felt nauseous. With great effort and a silent plea for help from God, she straightened and spoke as calmly as she could, "Bonnie, this is wrong. Stealing babies and selling them is a monstrous thing and framing your husband for it is also very wrong."

"What I do to Carlos Zorro is my affair!" Bonnie hissed, her lips white and compressed in the wavering candlelight. "He deserves all he will get! He dared to be unfaithful to me — Bonnie — who could have had her choice of many men!"

Her voice had reached an almost hysterical level. "Spending his time with a cheap dancing girl!" She spat viciously. "That's what I think of him — and his Violets — and that snob of a mother of his!" She spat again. "Trash — scum — fit to be walked into the ground of a pigsty! That's what I think of the Zorros! Foxes! Ha! They think they are so smart! Well, I, too, am a fox and much smarter than either of them! They will pay and pay dearly for the rest of their lives — *Don* Carlos and *Dona* Carlota! And you, too, Linn Randolph!"

Bonnie drew herself up to her full, diminutive stature. Her eyes glittered as she turned to Francesca. "Now, obey me! I will lift the lid. I want you to hold *Senora* Randolph's arms and *I* — who have no fear of death — will place the child in the coffin."

Francesca came forward reluctantly and moved around the table to stand behind

242

Linn. Bonnie followed her and raised the lid of the coffin. Linn saw that the inside of the casket was lined in luxurious white satin, with a small, lacy pillow.

Linn's heart lurched with physical pain, and her stomach felt as if it had been kicked. She had trouble breathing. Surely this was a nightmare from which she would presently awaken!

"Hold her arms," Bonnie ordered, and Linn felt Francesca's large hands clamp upon her arms like steel traps. Bonnie stepped forward and quickly removed the sleeping baby from Linn's arms. She didn't resist, fearful that Bobby would be hurt if she did, and also knowing, with an awful sense of desolation, that there was no use in resisting Francesca's powerful hands.

Bonnie carefully — almost reverently — placed Bobby on the soft satin inside the casket. The baby sighed in his sleep, turned onto his side, and put his thumb into his mouth. Linn could hear clearly the sound of his contented sucking.

Bonnie moved out of the circle of light and came back in a moment to lay a pale gold lily upon the sleeping child. "A proper funeral must have at least one flower," Bonnie said.

Linn felt as if her heart were being torn

from her body, bit by bit. "Dear Father," she whispered, "don't let this awful thing happen to me and my baby."

Bonnie moved gracefully to stand once more between the two black candles. She reminded Linn of a voodoo priestess. "Your prayers will do you no good," she said sarcastically. Linn had not known her prayer was audible, but she didn't care. "Now, close the casket, Linn."

"You can't do that!" Linn gasped. "Bobby will die!"

"No, he won't," Bonnie said emphatically. "This is a specially prepared casket that we have used several times to transport babies. There is ample ventilation and none has been harmed so far." A sly smile curved her delicate lips. "Bobby might be a bit frightened if he awoke, but he'll survive! Now lower the lid!"

"Never!" Francesca had released Linn's arms and she sprang forward to snatch Bobby from the casket. But Francesca grabbed her arms once more and hauled her up short.

"You may kiss your baby goodbye now," Bonnie said, a malevolent smile tugging at her lips. "It will be the last one — forever!"

"Is that so?" A cold voice spoke from the deep shadows behind Bonnie. Bonnie whirled about and Linn saw her face go ashy-white. Standing just at the edge of the shadows was Carlos Zorro, Bonnie's husband!

26

Linn backed away unconsciously from Carlos's handsome face. In the flickering candlelight, she could see that his hard, obsidian eyes were not upon her. She knew that he could be as cruel as Bonnie if he chose to be. She was vaguely aware that Francesca was also retreating unobtrusively into the shadows. Then the big maid vanished.

For a long tense moment there was no sound except for the clicking of the pendulum on a large grandfather clock in the room. Then Bonnie drew herself up to her proud, five feet height and said haughtily, "So you decided to leave Violeta and come back." The sound of her voice seemed to give her courage. "How wonderful to have you home! I suppose it is proper to give you a warm kiss, and welcome you back into my arms like a good Mexican wife should do!"

Carlos stepped closer; his black eyes glittered and his hands clenched. For a moment, Linn thought he was going to slap Bonnie. But he stood silently, staring into his wife's defiant eyes. Then he said almost gently, "If you were a good wife to me, I would not have to go looking for anyone else."

"If you were a good husband, you would have inspired better treatment from your wife," Bonnie shot back.

Carlos shrugged expressively and then said calmly, "What is this punishment you — or is it Adella? — have planned for me and my mother?"

"You will see," Bonnie said spitefully. "Now, it is late and I am leaving Guarida de los Zorros."

Bonnie stepped back around the table quickly. "Come, Linn, let us be going."

Suddenly a cultured voice spoke authoritatively behind Linn. "Bonnie, you are not taking *Dona* Randolph or her baby anywhere!"

When the voice spoke, Linn spun around. *Dona* Carlota was standing there. The silver in her dark hair sparkled in the candlelight. She was leaning on her black cane. Margarita stood at her elbow.

Carlota's dark eyes focused on Linn. "I am sorry to be so long in coming to your aid, but I had to wait until Carlos arrived. Then he had to stay out of sight — to collect some evidence to counteract the evidence Bonnie has planted to convict him."

"It was Carlos who was in his office last night — looking at the record book?" Linn asked.

"Yes, it was," Carlota said.

"I have been very busy," Carlos spoke up. "And I have all the evidence I need — on a recorder — to send my darling wife to prison for a very long time," Carlos finished mockingly from the other side of the little table with the white coffin on it.

Linn turned back and saw Carlos's derisive eyes resting upon his wife. Suddenly she felt pity for Bonnie. Her glowing complexion had gone grey and haggard in the dim light, and her eyes staring at Carlos seemed lustreless and old.

Carlos's voice held no pity or compassion. "I have already questioned my two men, Juan and Frank, and they confessed. They thought you — Adella," he said the name mockingly, were working under my orders, so I do not blame them. Juan said he dressed as an old man and spirited the kidnapped babies away in a donkey load of baskets or wood each time. Very ingenious!

"I couldn't figure out how Adella fit into

all of this until I listened in on your conversation with *Senora* Randolph last night — and recorded it all for the police."

Bonnie made a convulsive movement, but Carlos cut her off. His voice was harsh. "If Margarita had not sent a message to mother that she thought something strange was going on here at Guarida de los Zorros, she and I both would have been in jail by tomorrow, I expect. Isn't that right?"

He moved around the table and gripped Bonnie's arm. "And to think that I once thought I loved you! You are nothing but a monster!"

Suddenly Linn saw Bonnie's hand creep inside her silken blouse. "She's got a dagger!" Linn yelled.

But Bonnie's hand came out so quickly that it was difficult to see it move. A thin-bladed stiletto glittered wickedly in the light of the flickering black candles. Linn jumped back and bumped into Margarita who backed away, drawing Carlota with her.

Linn could see Bonnie's face clearly. A demented light glittered in her eyes, wild and eerie, as she lifted the dagger and lunged at Carlos with a crazed scream.

"You'll never live to enjoy your life with Violeta!"

Carlos leaped to the side but Bonnie was

quicker. Like a cat she pounced, plunging the slender blade into Carlos's chest with another insane scream of fury.

With a cry of anguish, Carlota tried to rush to Carlos's aid, but Margarita held her back with strong arms.

Carlos let out a strangled cry and grabbed for Bonnie, but she leaped away with a mocking cackle of triumph; the glittering dagger in her hand shone red in the flickering candlelight. Blood streamed down the front of Carlos's immaculate white shirt. Both of his hands clutched convulsively at his chest, and he slowly slumped to the floor.

Carlota again started to hobble toward her son's crumpled figure, but was halted by Bonnie's shriek, "Don't any of you move! I'll skewer the first one who makes a move to help this scoundrel!" Her laughter rang out again — high and crazed.

Linn shuddered. Bonnie's face was distorted into a hideous mask of hate and wrath. The dark blot that she had skillfully drawn at the corner of her left eye made her face look even more like that of an insane person.

Bonnie's wild eyes roved over the three silent women before her; a slow, malevolent smile came to her twisted lips as they stopped on Linn. "Linn, darling, it is too late. I am going to make you pay *now* for all the wrongs you have done to me."

She raised the slim, wicked blade high. As the gleaming blade slashed downward toward Linn's sleeping baby in the casket, Linn flung herself forward. She caught Bonnie's arm, and the dagger plunged into the satin lining not six inches from Bobby's face.

With a scream of rage, Bonnie whirled around and lunged at Linn. Linn dodged, heard the swish of the deadly weapon, and felt it tear through the material of her skirt. She launched herself at Bonnie before she could raise the stiletto again.

She was dimly aware that Bonnie had knocked over one of the long black candles on the end of the table. It rolled off, igniting the black casket cover that Linn had dropped to the floor minutes before. Out of the corner of her eye, Linn saw Margarita dash forward and stamp out the smoldering flames.

But Linn was too busy trying to take the knife from Bonnie's hand — and to keep from being stabbed by its keen blade — to heed much that was going on around her. Linn strove to put enough pressure on Bonnie's wrist to make her release it, but

Bonnie fought like an injured tigress.

Suddenly Bonnie brought up her knee and thrust it into Linn's stomach. Linn staggered back, her breath coming in painful gasps as black spots danced in front of her eyes.

Linn struggled to regain her breath; her harsh, labored breathing sounded loud to her own ears. Glancing up through dazed eyes, Linn saw Bonnie's arm again raise. Her dark, malicious eyes watched Linn, and a mocking smile formed on her twisted face as she slowly raised the blade high.

Summoning all the strength she could muster, Linn flung herself across the room at Bonnie. But before her plunge could carry her to Bonnie, the deadly stiletto came down and struck inside the small white casket.

Linn screamed. Her heart nearly burst from her body in awful pain and fear for her baby. But before she could reach the casket, Bonnie, as quick as a cobra, withdrew the knife and turned to face Linn again. She licked her lips in eager anticipation; a sadistic lust for revenge in her eyes.

Bonnie was between her and the little white coffin, crouched and waiting. The gleaming dagger was poised in her right hand. Tremors ran over Linn's body as she also crouched just beyond the reach of Bonnie's hands. Tears blurred her eyes. She must get to Bobby, and, yet, Bonnie and her deadly weapon stood between them!

Margarita! She must be in the room somewhere. Linn called frantically. "Margarita, please help my baby!" Her voice sounded shrill and hysterical to her own ears.

Bonnie backed up and turned her head toward the casket. As she did, Linn leaped at her, managing to get one strong hand around Bonnie's fist that held the dagger. Instantly, Bonnie became like a wild animal, raking Linn with her fingernails and writhing to tear Linn's grip away from the hand that clutched the stiletto.

Suddenly, Bonnie grabbed a handful of Linn's hair and pulled violently, drawing Linn toward her. Then she sank her small, sharp teeth into Linn's left shoulder. The pain from both the hair pulling and the bite were intense, and Linn almost lost her hold on Bonnie's dagger hand. But with grim determination and a desperate knowledge that the stiletto would be in her heart if she released Bonnie's wrist, Linn hung on as the pain raged in her head and shoulder.

Bonnie's teeth found their mark again in Linn's upper left arm and pain ripped through her flesh, nearly paralyzing the arm. In agony, Linn threw her body against Bonnie, and both went down hard. Now Linn had the advantage. She was taller and heavier than Bonnie and when they fell, Bonnie took the brunt of the fall.

The black candles did not shed much light on the floor, and Linn felt more than saw that she still retained her hold on Bonnie's wrist. She struggled to pin Bonnie down with her body while using both hands in an attempt to take away her dagger.

For a few seconds, Bonnie seemed stunned from the fall, and then she was again a raging tigress — with superhuman strength, it seemed — writhing, biting, and clawing. Linn smashed Bonnie's wrist against the floor once but her grip held. Then they were rolling and struggling together on the floor. As they struggled, from Bonnie's mouth issued unintelligible, savage sounds. They made Linn's blood run cold, and her heart constrict with dread. There seemed little doubt that she was fighting with a woman gone mad!

Suddenly, Bonnie rolled free and wrenched the dagger away from Linn's hand. Instantly she was on her feet, standing over Linn with the wickedly gleaming blade drawn back in her hand. Her hideous laugh of triumph rang out as she began to bring the dagger down.

Linn tried to roll away. Bonnie's lithe figure followed her, laughing mockingly. Linn tried to trip Bonnie, but she danced lightly away and then again drew back the flashing stiletto.

"Lord Jesus, please help me!" Linn cried aloud.

Just then, glaring lights filled the room. Bonnie stood rigid with surprise for a second, and then with a wild scream, she plunged the knife downward. But Linn was not there! She had rolled to the side, and the dagger stabbed into the carpeted floor inches from her shoulder.

Uniformed men rushed into the room. Bonnie tried to tear the dagger from the floor, but before she could, two policemen grabbed her arms and drew them back to handcuff them. But she became a raving savage — kicking, clawing, biting, and shrieking insanely. A third policeman had to come to their assistance before Bonnie's slim, shapely hands could be restrained. But even then she refused to be subdued.

She continued to kick and bite until her legs were pinioned together with manacles. A policeman laid her face down on the floor, but she filled the close air with maniacal screams until someone tied a cloth about her mouth.

An officer gently helped Linn to her feet. With a cry, Linn ran to the little coffin. The blanket-wrapped object lay silent and still. Frantically, Linn reached for the still form. Her heart was quaking with fear as she lifted it — and then she threw it down in shocked surprise. The object was fluffy and had no weight to it! Where was her son?

Linn's eyes swept the room — searching, searching. Where was her baby? Who had taken him out of the casket?

The room was swarming with uniformed men. Linn saw several men kneeling on the floor about Carlos. Carlota was also there, sitting on the floor next to her son, stroking his cheek. A man who looked like a doctor was working on him.

The policeman who had lifted Linn to her feet was now at her side. He spoke in perfect English. "I think you need some medical attention, too, as soon as the doctor gets *Don* Carlos ready to transport to the hospital."

Surprised, Linn looked down at her own body and suddenly realized her arms, shoulder, and face throbbed from the many bites and scratches she had received. "I'm all right, but I can't find my baby! He may be dying — or-or already. . . ." She couldn't say it!

Puzzled, the policeman said, "Baby? There is no baby here that I know of. Where. . . ."

Impatiently, Linn broke in, "Bonnie stabbed him with h-her dagger!" Her voice broke on a sob. "H-he was here in the casket."

Suddenly a voice spoke her name, and Linn whirled around. Then she was in Clay's arms, crying hysterically. "B-Bobby's hurt — m-maybe even dead — and I can't find him."

Clay held her close, caressing her hair fiercely. "Bobby's all right, honey. He doesn't have a scratch!"

Linn drew back and looked into Clay's face in astonishment, "He is? Where — who — are you sure? How do you know?" she stammered.

"I don't know what happened, but I do know that a maid called Margarita has him in the next room, and he is perfectly all right!"

Just then Linn heard a soft voice at her elbow. "Is this what you are looking for?"

Linn turned and saw Margarita's warm, smiling face; cuddled against her shoulder, sleeping peacefully, was Bobby!

Linn ran exploring, loving fingers along the length of the sleeping form of her son and stroked his pink cheeks before she took him almost reverently from Margarita's arms. He stirred slightly, yawned, and arched his body before settling himself into the curve of his mother's arm.

"What happened?" she asked Margarita, wonderingly. "I thought Bonnie had stabbed him and that he was hurt — if not w-worse!"

Margarita laughed softly. "When the candle fell over and the cloth on the floor caught fire, I stamped out the flames. I was right at the side of the casket. Bonnie was so busy trying to stab you that I snatched the baby out of the casket and ran next door and put him 'way back in the corner of a closet. I brought his blanket back, wrapped it about a soft pillow, and put it in the casket."

She giggled. "Do you know, he never even woke up through everything?"

"We owe our baby's life to you and your quick thinking," Linn said gratefully. "How is Carlos?"

"He is badly hurt and has lost a lot of blood, but the doctor thinks he'll live. The dagger missed his heart. Carlota went to him when I snatched the baby, and she pressed a ball of cloth against the wound to slow the bleeding. I got some ice from the little refrigerator in Bonnie's bar and made an ice-pack for the wound."

Turning to face Clay, Linn asked, "How did you and everyone else happen to come — even a doctor?"

"Through Jake and Penny's sleuthing. They found out that Luisa had the license plate number of the car that took you away," Clay said. "The police found out that the car belonged to Carlos Zorro. They prepared to move in on the house, but before they could get organized, they received a call from Carlos urging them to come quickly. He said Bonnie was responsible for the kidnappings and that she was holding you and Bobby, as well as Luisa's baby, captive.

"But he almost waited too long. When we arrived, Carlos had already been wounded and," Clay shuddered visibly, "one of the policemen said Bonnie was standing over you with a dagger drawn back when they turned on the light."

Linn shuddered. "I think Bonnie would have killed us all if the police had not come when they did!"

"We didn't know what we would find here," Clay continued, "so we brought a doctor and an ambulance. But it took some talking before the police chief would let me come."

Clay put his arms about Linn and Bobby and drew them close. "Only the Lord got us here in time. I'm so thankful to Him that I still have a wife and son!"

27

Attendants were carrying Carlos out The doctor, a small trim man, came to Linn's side. "I would like you to come to the hospital, too. Those bites need attention, and I would like to check you over for other injuries."

Linn protested, but Clay added his voice to the doctor's and in the end, Linn went.

Much later, in a large hospital in Veracruz, Linn's injuries were cleaned, and she was given a tetanus shot. Bobby was also checked by a doctor and declared to be in perfect condition.

It was dawn when Clay and Linn approached *Dona* Carlota and Margarita in the surgery waiting room. Carlota's patrician face was pale and dark circles outlined her tired eyes, but she welcomed them warmly. "I haven't had a chance to offer my thanks properly," she told Linn. "If you had not warned Carlos, he might not be with us now."

"How is he?" Linn asked.

"Carlos is in surgery, but we have a team of good doctors, and they are optimistic. Carlos is in excellent health and the dagger missed his heart," Carlota replied. "Are you and Bobby all right?"

"We're fine," Linn said. "I just have a few bites, scratches, and bruises. And thanks to your Margarita, Bobby is perfect!"

Clay spread a blanket on the long couch and gently laid his son down. Bobby's eyelids fluttered. He stretched, stuck a fat thumb in his mouth, and curled into a contented ball.

"He's a fine baby," Carlota said. She paused and then said apologetically, "I know you are tired, *Dona* Linn, but something I overheard you tell Bonnie puzzles me. You told her she need not fear death if she knew God. And that God did not require a lot from us."

Her fine brow wrinkled. "I could scarcely believe the courage with which you faced Bonnie during the gruesome little ceremony she had planned for you and your baby. We heard it all. You have something I do not possess. I was amazed at the gentle spirit you showed as you tried to persuade Bonnie

— an enemy who was doing all she could to make you suffer — to accept forgiveness of her sins and to turn to Christ."

Carlota's dark eyes filled with tears. "Bonnie did not want God's forgiveness, but I do! I have always desired to really know God, but I never knew how to find Him. Always I have felt that God was frowning upon me, and I have felt so ugly and dirty before Him.

"I have done all I know to do and still I have no peace. I am old — and I am terrified of death because I will face a God of wrath. Is it really as simple as you told Bonnie? To obtain the forgiveness of God?" Her voice sank to a whisper of desperate longing.

A lump as big as a pineapple seemed to fill Linn's throat, and she had to swallow twice before she could answer. Leaning forward she took Carlota's soft, wrinkled hand and spoke softly. "It's as simple as that! When I was very young, some things happened to me that caused intense bitterness in my heart. I felt I had been deeply wronged, and I became very self-centered, sarcastic, and hateful. Then a doctor and his sweet wife befriended me and introduced me to their friend, Jesus.

"I invited Him into my heart and life,

asked forgiveness for my wickedness, and gave Him the reins to my life." Linn laughed softly. "He took away the bitterness and made me a new person. I have not always pleased Him, but God forgives me when I ask and restores peace and joy to my life."

"And your husband also has this peace." Carlota looked at Clay. "It is in his eyes just as it is in yours."

Clay spoke earnestly. "Yes I do, but I have not always known God's forgiveness and joy. I considered myself an intellectual and was not even certain I believed in God. Certainly not in one who was concerned with the puny affairs of man."

Clay stopped; his hazel eyes mirrored painful memories. "I became angry with my wife and stupidly sent her away from my house. Then I realized I had made a mistake and tried to find her and bring her home. But Linn had taken me at my word, and though I searched frantically, I could not find her.

"Finally, when I was at the lowest point of my entire life, in desperation I turned to God for help, and I found that help. I had only to reach out and God was there! God not only forgave me and filled my life with meaning, but He gave me back my wife."

Clay reached for Linn's hand and

squeezed it. "We are both strong-willed, and sometimes we have some pretty stiff disagreements, but God has given us a deeper love for each other than I ever thought possible! I would recommend trusting God with your life to anyone!"

"Tell me again what I must do to find this peace with God," Carlota said.

Margarita had sat withdrawn from the conversation, her face like a mask. Suddenly, she jumped up, muttered something about needing to get some water, and hurried away.

Carlota laughed softly. "Margarita obviously thinks I am a little *loco*. But even if I am branded a fanatic, I must have peace in my troubled heart. If I had had what you two seem to have, perhaps my Carlos would not have followed in the steps of his half-outlaw father. But I could not impart something to my son that I did not possess."

She reiterated resolutely, "Now, tell me what I must do to obtain this forgiveness — and peace and joy."

Linn's voice quickened with eagerness, "Just acknowledge your need of Christ. Tell God that you believe that His Son, Jesus, died for your sins and that you want Jesus to come into your life and forgive you and cleanse you from your sin. Then simply believe that God meant what He said, and thank Him for making you His child! That's all there is to it!"

Carlota hesitated. "I-I do not know how to talk to God — like that."

"We will help you," Clay said gently. "The words you use are not that important; God knows if you genuinely want to give your life to Him."

Clay took one of her frail hands in his and Linn the other. Together, they prayed. Carlota, falteringly at first, asked God's forgiveness and surrendered her life to Him. When they were finished, she looked first at Clay and then Linn. "How do I know if He heard me? I certainly do not feel any different."

"You must believe that God has forgiven you," Linn said earnestly. "A new feeling will usually follow, but whether it does or not, God's Word is true. You are now a child of God!"

"I am?" Carlota said it like a small child, wonderingly but also questioningly.

"You are!" Linn said confidently. "And the more you affirm that you are, the more it will become a reality to you."

"I am a child of God," Carlota said slowly, as if she were savoring the words. "I am a child of God. I am forgiven — because

God's Word says I am. I am a child of God."

As she repeated the words, they began to take on a confident tone. Her eyes began to shine. Excitedly, she said, "I do believe! I really *am* a child of God!"

"Of course you are!" Clay affirmed with a smile. "The Bible says that we believe with our hearts, but that it is important for us to speak our newborn faith with our mouths. Personally, I think our ears hear our words and then they sink deep down into our souls and generate genuine faith."

At that moment a man in a white jacket came hurrying down the hospital corridor. *Dona* Carlota stood up quickly, leaning on her black cane. The man took Carlota's thin hand and pressed it, speaking in rapid Spanish. Carlota asked questions a couple of times, and he answered her. Then, bowing slightly, the man went striding back down the hallway.

"Carlos is out of surgery. The doctors feel he will make a complete recovery. He must remain in the hospital for awhile, but he is going to be fine." Tears glistened in her dark eyes, "I am so thankful to God!"

"What of Bonnie?" Linn asked somewhat hesitantly.

Carlota spoke sadly. "She was put in the mental health section of the hospital and heavily sedated. Restraints have been placed on her, and she is under guard.

"The doctor did not know if she will be rational when she regains consciousness. If she is, she will be placed in jail, of course. If not. . . ." Carlota let the words trail off. "It is so sad for one as beautiful as my daughter-in-law to be so consumed with hate that it affects everyone around her. I only wish she could know the peace I have just found!"

28

The Molinas's *corredore* and patio-garden were ablaze with lights. Dinner was over and everyone, replete with good Mexican cooking, settled back to enjoy the balmy Veracruz evening. The air was filled with the heady perfume from Alicia's flower garden. From somewhere nearby, a husky male voice could be heard serenading his sweetheart. The guitar music and haunting love song seemed to cast a bewitching spell over the evening.

Eric Ford had arrived in Veracruz three days before, and it had been almost a week since Linn, Bobby, and Manuelito had been rescued.

Curled up in a comfortable, cushioned chair, Linn smiled to herself as she relived the happy reunion between Luisa, Jorge, and their little son. Luisa's plain face had glowed with such a radiance that she was beautiful.

She glanced up and saw Clay's warm,

hazel eyes on her. He reached for her hand and leaned close to her ear, "Have I told you today that I love you, Linn Randolph?"

"Not over a hundred times; you can tell me again."

Across the room Jake spoke in his booming voice, "How's that Zorro guy?"

"He's mending so well that *Dona* Carlota expects to take him home in a few days," Esteban answered.

"But Bonnie's case is pathetic," Linn said sadly. "Carlota said she is so violent that she has to be kept sedated and in a padded cell to keep her from harming herself or someone else."

"Vengeance is a cruel master," Clay said thoughtfully. "Bonnie has given herself over to hate until it has destroyed her, it seems."

"Do the doctors think Bonnie will ever recover?" Kate asked.

"The doctors say it is too early to tell," Linn replied. "They feel she will be under treatment for a long, long time, and she may never be well again."

"I just shrivel up inside when I think how close she came to murdering you and Bobby," Penny said, shuddering. "And to think that Bonnie had already sold Bobby to a wealthy couple in Australia just like he was a piece of merchandise!"

"At least the police found a good record so they were able to locate and return all the kidnapped babies," Josie said.

"Chief Sanchez told me that two of the couples let their babies stay with their adoptive parents," Jake said. "That's what I call real love! They couldn't give them what the new parents could and wanted the best for their kids!"

"Say, Eric, how about a sing-a-long," Esteban said, breaking the somber mood that seemed to be descending. Everyone enthusiastically added their voices to his.

Josie's husband, Eric, a crooked grin on his good-looking face, went to get his ukulele and soon had everyone singing in happy abandonment. As usual, he asked for volunteers to sing or in some way add to the entertainment. Josie sang an old ballad in her pure-as-a-bell voice. Eric did a couple of funny songs from the 1940s and 1950s with Clay's bass and Josie's soprano harmonizing. Even Alicia and Esteban sang — shyly but well — a song in Spanish. Both Linn and Kate declined, but Jake sang the old cowboy song, "Strawberry Roan," with much more enthusiasm than talent, and was roundly applauded.

"It's your turn now, Penny and Alfred," Eric said with a big grin.

Penny and Alfred were sitting together in a cushioned swing. The bright lights shimmered on Penny's long silvery hair and turned Alfred's dark head into polished mahogany. They made a handsome picture. They were scarcely ever seen apart these days.

Penny declared that she was no singer, but Alfred said he had a song. Asking Eric to accompany him on the ukulele, Alfred sang — in a light, pleasant baritone — a song in Spanish. As he sang, his eyes never left Penny's face. When he had finished, Penny clapped her hands enthusiastically, as did everyone else.

"Where did you learn a song in Spanish?" she asked in surprise.

"Since I have been here," he said, obviously very pleased with himself.

"You know, *Senorita* Penny, that you are being courted, don't you?" Esteban said, his dark eyes twinkling. "That is a song of love that our young men in Mexico sing to declare their love to their sweethearts."

Penny, her pale pointed face suddenly rosy, turned quick eyes to Alfred's face. His face took on a slightly rosy flush, too, but his dark eyes met hers steadily. He started to say something, but Luisa arrived at that moment.

She came quickly out into the loggia and moved to where Penny and Alfred were sitting together. "A telephone call, *Senorita* Peeny." At Penny's questioning look, she continued, "The same young man who has called you two times before."

Penny hesitated. She had refused to talk to Bart before when he had called. *Perhaps he is going to make himself a nuisance if I don't talk to him,* she thought.

Jake spoke up from across the room, "Penny, do you want me to send him packing?"

Penny glanced at Jake and grinned. A short while ago she would have let Jake know, in no uncertain terms, that she didn't want his interference. Now, she said, "Thanks, but I think I had better take care of this."

Penny rose to go and saw the anxious expression on Kate's face. She touched her lightly on the arm as she passed her and said softly, "Don't worry, mother. I can handle it."

She was gone for several moments. When she returned she took her place next to Alfred without a word. There was a slight pause in the conversation, and then Eric again started a rousing sing-a-long which everyone joined into.

Everyone but Alfred. He leaned over and asked Penny, "Could we talk — away from the others?"

Penny searched his serious face for a moment and then agreed.

Taking her hand, Alfred rose and led her out into the patio-garden, past the fountain, to a black wrought iron bench, set in seclusion behind a screen of bougainvillea. Drawing Penny down beside him, Alfred said peremptorily, "I guess Bart wanted to make up?"

"Yes."

"Well — what did you tell him?"

Penny looked up coyly through golden eyelashes. Her green eyes were dancing with mischief. "Why do you want to know?"

Alfred looked exasperated. "Is it over between you two? For good?"

"Why?" Penny repeated.

Alfred's face turned pink, and his brown eyes darkened, "Don't tease me, Penny! You know I'm serious." He looked miserable. "I have to know how I stand with you! Do you care for me at all?"

Penny's expressive, pointed face sobered. "I told Bart the truth. I had never loved him; he was just part of my rebellion against Jake and mother. I told him that he was fun to be with, but that even if I had loved him, I would never marry someone who uses drugs."

"How did he take it?"

"He promised never to touch drugs again. He said he didn't believe for a minute that I didn't love him, and declared that mother and Jake had influenced me against him. He urged me to see him when I get home and let him prove that I loved him."

"Are you going to?"

"My — my, but you are inquisitive! Of course I don't plan to see him again! You don't think I'm crazy, do you?"

"No, I don't! I think you are the sweetest and most wonderful girl in all the world," Alfred said softly, his voice husky with emotion. His dark eyes were warm. "I needed to know that you no longer cared for Bart. I love you and have ever since I first set eyes on you five years ago."

He lifted Penny's hand to his lips and kissed her palm. "Esteban was right, you know. I learned that song to sing it to you. It's an old Mexican custom to serenade your beloved, and I wanted you to know that you are that to me."

He swallowed hard and then blurted out, "I nearly lost you by not telling you before how I felt. You see, I was waiting until I could offer you some security. But I will be out of college in a few months and chances are good that I have a job in the research department of a large company as a marine biologist. Penny, do you think you could learn to love me?"

Penny's heart constricted with a strange but wonderful feeling. "I think I have always loved you, too, Alfred," she said tremulously. "But I also think we should be sure. You have college to finish, and then you will need to establish yourself in your new job. We are both very young, and we have lots of time. Couldn't we just enjoy dating and writing and give ourselves some space to grow up a little more before we make any definite commitments?"

"Not only the prettiest girl in town but the smartest, too." Alfred was grinning, then he sobered. "But there is no doubt in my mind of how I feel about you." He leaned over and kissed Penny almost reverently. "I've dreamed of doing that," he said huskily, "but didn't know if I would ever have the nerve."

Silently, Penny gripped his hand, her green eyes filled with a peaceful joy. Hand in hand, they walked back to join the others.